"You're right. I'm not consistent."

There, Angela had admitted it. "I'm tempted, but I'm not going to ask you in. I got myself into one hellish mess years ago by . . . by letting myself get carried away." She drew in a deep breath. "I'm never going to let that happen again."

Kent was suddenly very quiet, his eyes watching her. Assessing. Looking for weaknesses. She shivered.

"Haven't you blown this out of proportion, Angela?" His voice was very reasonable. She decided it must be the voice he used to negotiate land deals. "We're not talking about permanence here. We're talking about you and me and what's unfinished between us."

She met his eyes. "Making love?"

"Put whatever name you want on it." He shrugged. "I want to go to bed with you, you want it, too. If you're afraid there's more to it than that, you can quit worrying."

VANESSA GRANT started writing her first romance at the age of twelve and hasn't forgotten the excitement of having a love story come to life on paper. After spending four years refitting the forty-six-foot yacht they live on, she and her husband, Brian, and their teenage son set sail south to Mexico along the North American West Coast. Vanessa divides her time between her writing, sailing and exploring the harbors of the Pacific Coast. She often writes her love stories on her portable computer while anchored in remote inlets. Vanessa says, "I believe in love and in happy endings."

Books by Vanessa Grant

HARLEQUIN PRESENTS
1234—AWAKENING DREAMS
1264—WILD PASSAGE
1289—TAKING CHANCES
1322—SO MUCH FOR DREAMS
1386—ONE SECRET TOO MANY
1426—THE TOUCH OF LOVE

HARLEQUIN ROMANCE
2888—THE CHAUVINIST

Don't miss any of our special offers. Write to us at the following address for information on our newest releases.

Harlequin Reader Service
P.O. Box 1397, Buffalo, NY 14240
Canadian address: P.O. Box 603,
Fort Erie, Ont. L2A 5X3

VANESSA GRANT

Angela's Affair

Harlequin Books

TORONTO • NEW YORK • LONDON
AMSTERDAM • PARIS • SYDNEY • HAMBURG
STOCKHOLM • ATHENS • TOKYO • MILAN
MADRID • WARSAW • BUDAPEST • AUCKLAND

For Nonie
Friend and craftswoman
Thank you for sharing so much

Harlequin Presents first edition September 1992
ISBN 0-373-11490-7

Original hardcover edition published in 1991
by Mills & Boon Limited

ANGELA'S AFFAIR

CHAPTER ONE

ANGELA lifted her foot off the sewing-machine pedal, swung her chair around and reached for the telephone receiver, one hand stretched back to anchor the canvas fisherman's shirt she was sewing. She blinked against the glare of the morning sun through the window, her green eyes widening as the double doors to the shop burst open.

Her father-in-law Harvey exploded into the shop, his movements rough and sharp, his jaw clenched. He was normally soft-spoken, quiet-moving, a haven for other people's storms. Yet right now his lean body was tensed like an overloaded spring.

Angela put the receiver to her ear and announced, "Dalton Welding and Canvas. Good morning," then put her hand over the mouthpiece and whispered urgently, "Dad, what's wrong?"

In her ear, a woman's voice was framing a long, complicated explanation. Angela hardly heard it, distracted by the impossible sight of Harvey with his graying hair wild around his head and his eyes jerking everywhere. He planted both hands on the counter and demanded, "Where is she? Where's Charlotte?"

The voice in her ear said, "... survey of merchants in Port Townsend, to ascertain their satisfaction with insurance serv——"

"No," she said firmly. "I don't want to take part in a survey."

"The results of this survey will be used to——"

"I'm not interested," Angela insisted.

7

Harvey blinked, his breathing still heavy. "What? Angie, if you know where she is, you've got to tell me. I've got to——"

She lifted her hand to silence him and the canvas slid to the floor. Damn! Twenty fishermen's shirts, ten with red trim and ten with blue, and this was only number eleven. Number eleven, and it seemed doomed from the beginning. In her right ear, the insurance voice turned reasonable and overly patient just as Harvey started shouting.

"Angie! Did you hear me? Charlotte's gone! She's not at her boat!"

"Yes—— No, I wasn't talking to you! No, we *don't* want to take part in the survey!"

Sweetly persistent, the voice inquired, "Are you insured with a local firm?"

"Yes," Angela responded automatically. Harvey pounded the counter with his fist. "Dad, she's probably—— Listen, if that's one of the questions in the survey, we don't——"

Behind her, the window to the welding shop slid open and Barney shouted, "Angie? Did you remember to order those stainless fittings for the bows?"

In her ear, the woman's voice probed softly, "Is the amount of your fire coverage greater than a hundred thousand dollars? Or less?"

Through the shop-front window, behind the display of canvas bags, Angela could see a middle-aged couple crossing the gravel street, coming this way. All she wanted was a quiet morning to get the fishermen's shirts done, but the customers were already coming and Harvey looked as if he might explode at any moment, while Barney in his coveralls was crowding through the doorway from the shop, asking again about the fittings.

The survey-taker repeated her question.

Angela sighed. "Look, I don't have time for your survey. I——"

Harvey slammed the counter. "Angie!" His thick salt-and-pepper eyebrows drew together over worried brown eyes. "Hang up and listen to me! Charlotte isn't on her boat. It's all locked up and she's gone."

"Gone shopping?" No, if it was a shopping trip, Charlotte would have stopped here at the shop to say hello.

He exploded, "Gone! The shades are all pulled down over her portholes. Her dinghy's up on deck, and the guy in the next slip said Charlotte left at dawn this morning, carrying a suitcase."

Two months ago the middle-aged Charlotte had sailed into the quiet ship-building town of Port Townsend. A burst of sunlight, Harvey had said. He had been lonely since his beloved Anna had died, but he had started smiling because of Charlotte, even laughing.

Now Barney leaned on the desk beside Angela, his welding mask pushed up. "What's this about Charlotte? Angie, did those fittings come? Get on the blower, would you, and follow up? I can't do this job without them."

The voice in her ear was repeating the question about coverage. Angela snapped, "Listen, I don't want to take part in your survey. I'm hanging up." She winced as she put the receiver down. She *never* hung up on people.

"The fittings——"

Harvey leaned over the counter, his face haggard and older than it should be. "Do you know where she went? Angie? Did you know she was going?"

"No, of course not." She had been afraid of it, though. Hadn't Charlotte confessed to Angela that running was the only way she could handle complications?

Angela waved one arm toward a box at the end of the counter and pushed her other hand through unruly auburn curls. "Right there, Barney. That box. The UPS man just delivered it five minutes ago."

Barney grabbed the box and strode away toward the shop. "Aren't you going to say thank you?" Angela called after him.

When Barney got involved in a job, nothing else mattered. He was very much like his father. Both were tall and good-looking in a brown-haired, brown-eyed fashion, although Harvey's browns were fading into attractive gray, while Barney's nose had once been broken by his older brother Ben.

Angela remembered the fight that had broken Barney's nose. It had happened the night before Ben asked her to marry him, Barney's attempt to protect a seventeen-year-old Angela from his wild older brother. As if Barney were her older brother, protecting his kid sister. As if Ben had been a stranger. Angela hadn't wanted protecting, had been terrified when Ben lost his temper and ploughed his fist into Barney's face.

But she had loved Ben.

It had not been a quiet, planned wedding, but an elopement, an exciting adventure. So long ago. Ben was hardly even a memory now, although his family was her family, while she had not seen her own parents in years. Sometimes she tried to close her eyes and picture Ben's face, but it was years since she had been able to make an image of him in her mind. The bitterness was gone, but she could still feel the echo of the pain. Ben Dalton was the only man she had ever loved, and she had loved him with an impulsive, abandoned passion.

Until the end, when he had left her alone. Doubly alone, because she had lost the baby too.

The couple outside stopped to look at something in the window, the woman pointing and her bearded partner frowning. Harvey let out a long breath that seemed to leave him limp and worried. "Angie, do you have any idea where she can be?"

Angela remembered the day Charlotte Ferguson had first come into Dalton Welding and Canvas. On impulse, she had said, asking about having a cockpit dodger made for her boat. Angela had liked her on sight, while Harvey had immediately decided that, although he had been semiretired for three years, *he* would go down to the boat with Angela to do the estimate, instead of Barney.

Barney, already overworked in the summer season, had laughed and warned, "Go ahead, but watch out for her. She's a fifty-year-old bombshell. She'll sting you." It had been meant as a joke. Harvey had been widowed three years, had not once even hinted that he might put another woman in Anna's place.

Only now Harvey was leaning on the counter, worrying, "Do you think she's hurt? Sick? I'd better phone the hospital."

"Didn't you say she took a suitcase?" Angela hated to see Harvey like this, hurting. "Dad, did you put the pressure on her last night?"

He ran a work-hardened hand through his unruly hair. Usually he wore it shorter, tidier, but a few weeks ago Angela had overheard Charlotte telling him that she liked it curling and longish. Harvey had canceled his barber's appointment. Now he confessed, "I asked her again. To marry me."

Oh, Lord. Angela remembered last weekend when Charlotte had taken Angela sailing, claiming she needed a woman's company for a while. There were more than twenty years between the two women, but last weekend, anchored in Mystery Bay, Charlotte had revealed secrets she had never told anyone else.

"She's run away," Harvey decided bleakly. "Why would she run away from me?"

Angela covered Harvey's restless hand with her own. "Dad, take it easy. Maybe she wanted to be alone for a while. To think." Except that Angela knew about Charlotte's flights. Coming back wasn't part of the deal.

He swallowed. "She paid the boat moorage until Sunday. She'll come back by then, won't she? She wouldn't just abandon her boat."

Kent Ferguson received the telegram on Thursday morning. A message from Charlotte, the last thing he needed in the midst of trying to decide whether to exercise his option on the Wimbley property!

When Patricia slipped quietly into Kent's office, he pushed the surveyor's report aside with a decisive motion of his long-fingered hands. Everything about him was long and lean and orderly—his body, spare and hard with no extra flesh over its six feet, clothed in a dark, tailored three-piece suit; his face, frowning as he watched his assistant approaching with an envelope in her hand; his hair, cut medium length, blond gone dark, waving and precisely controlled. Behind him, the skyscrapers of the Vancouver financial district were clear and beautiful against the blue of Coal Harbour. As usual, he was too busy to notice or to care.

"Patricia, get Emerson on the phone. Tell him I want to meet with him this afternoon."

She cautioned, "This telegram just came. Do you want to check it first?" Her voice was just as it should be to fit into his world, clear and precise and efficient. She was thirty and looked older, dressed quietly but tastefully. Her looks were much like her voice, smooth, dark-haired, tidy to the point of dullness. She had just arrived in the office for the day, and he did not need his watch to know it was precisely nine o'clock.

It was a commercial telegram, not a tear-sheet from their office telex. That meant Charlotte, not business.

He frowned, feeling the irritation his older sister always brought, and muttered, "You'd think she could at least phone... Go ahead trying to get Emerson. Whatever mess she's in this time can wait until I've seen Emerson."

Five years since he had seen Charlotte face-to-face. He frowned, staring at the unopened telegram, remembering the day he had come home to the sounds of Charlotte and his mother, their voices raised in an argument that ceased the moment he closed the door. He had caught only a few words, senseless words in Charlotte's raised voice, and his mother saying sharply, "No! Never! If you do, I'll..."

After that, there had been that ominous tension in the air until the day of his father's funeral. Then Charlotte had left, characteristically, without telling anyone where she was going.

Although they had never been close, Kent missed his sister—a weakness he was not about to admit to anyone.

Sometimes he thought about getting married, bringing a woman, a lover, into the forbidding house where his mother lived. Then he wondered what kind of woman he could find who would be able to handle his mother, and doubted if it was worth the bother. He was content with his life. He had a suite on Sunset Beach, not far from the office, and that was more his home than the big old family house on Marine Drive.

Most of his life was tied up in his work, but occasionally there was a woman. Dinner and dancing, then back to his apartment, but he never asked a woman to stay over for the night. If a man was going to sleep with a lover, wake with her soft in his arms, he should feel something more than Kent ever had.

He would have liked children, but he had never found anyone he wanted to marry. His sister would say he had never fallen in love, but, looking at Charlotte's life, love seemed more a disaster than a delight. She herself had left at least two men at the altar, always shying away from commitment at the last moment.

As for his love life, the fault was in him, he knew. He suspected that he would never care enough about any woman to make even the smallest sacrifice of his business affairs. Now, dropping his blue eyes to the envelope, he remembered his older sister's voice, years ago, accusing him of being a coldhearted bastard.

Perhaps he *was* cold, but better that than the way Charlotte flitted from one crisis to another, leaving destruction in her wake and always expecting someone else to bail her out. For years it had been Dad who straightened out Charlotte's messes, but Kent had taken over the chore, just as he had taken over the rest of the Ferguson empire when his father died. Charlotte was sixteen years older, but Kent had always been the responsible one. He got the work, including dealing with her discarded men, while Charlotte spent the money and enjoyed the freedom.

Sometimes he felt like shaking her, but it was pointless. If she was ever going to grow up, it would have happened a long time ago.

He frowned over the words of the telegram, wondering what kind of mess was hidden in them. When it had been Dad looking after her problems, Charlotte had telephoned. Now she used telegrams, probably because her relationship with Kent had never been comfortable.

He reached for the intercom. "Patricia, where's Port Townsend?"

There was a pause while Patricia consulted one of the reference books she kept by her desk, then, "In the States, at the entrance to Puget Sound."

"Near Seattle?"

"More or less. About sixty miles north, connection by bridges and ferries. There's an airport."

The last time he heard from Charlotte, she had been in Sitka, Alaska, although he couldn't imagine why even Charlotte would be crazy enough to take her sailboat to Alaska. Why not Mexico or Tahiti, somewhere *warm*? But then, he never had understood her, had thought she was crazy when she bought the boat.

Why couldn't she act like the middle-aged woman she was? Settle down and join a few clubs, play bridge and stop behaving like an overgrown flower child! If she had to flit around, the least she could do was leave her loose ends in a city like Toronto or Seattle, somewhere he had connections. Port Townsend, for God's sake!

"Patricia, tell Wayne I'll want the Lear ready at dawn tomorrow for a flight to Port Townsend. Arrange a rental car to meet me. Call my mother and tell her I won't be able to make dinner tomorrow night."

He usually delegated Charlotte's tasks to the lawyers, but they wouldn't have a clue what to do about a sailboat abandoned in a marina in Port Townsend. If Charlotte wanted a damned boat, why didn't she look after it?

Kent left Charlotte's boat unlocked and went ashore to search for the marina office. He didn't have much luck there, although he did get the name of a Seattle firm that specialized in boat deliveries. He had left his briefcase with his cellular telephone down on the boat, so he stopped at a pay phone that was crammed up against the wall of a shipbuilder's shed and dialed, using his calling card.

Behind him, Port Townsend rose against the cloudy sky, a hillside dotted with old Victorian mansions—picturesque, peaceful. Kent thought vaguely of digging up someone in town and doing some checking on property prices, but he had a sailboat to contend with first.

As he waited for the call to go through, he watched an old gray van park beside his rental car. The driver's door swung open, just missing the Chevette, and Kent winced.

A girl got out of the van. She was dressed in something casual, pants and blouse that were probably cotton. She reached back into the van and his eyes were caught as her pants stretched tight over feminine thighs and buttocks. When she straightened, balancing an irregular bundle of dark blue fabric, he decided that she was not strictly a girl. A woman. Late twenties, and she would be a knockout in a green evening gown with that soft reddish hair and those passionately wild curls tumbled everywhere.

She gave the hair a shake and twitched her hip to push the door of the van closed. Firm muscles and soft white skin. She twisted to balance the bundle of fabric on her hip and he added ''very female curves'' to his mental inventory.

A short, stocky man wearing coveralls hurried past her, then stopped and held out his hands as if to take her bundle. She laughed and shook her head. A mechanic, Kent thought, assessing the man out of habit. Probably good at his job, but inclined to take a few minutes off here and there for socializing. And the girl——

Maybe it had been too long since he had been involved with a woman. He watched the girl's back as she walked toward the ramp, feeling his pulses stir and his body harden.

''Smarten up, Ferguson,'' he muttered to himself as the ringing sound began in his ear. He had more important things to do than stand in a telephone booth, feeling a crazy stirring for a woman he would never see again.

With any luck, tonight he would be home in Vancouver. Then, after he had finished going over those contractor's bids, he would call Sheila or Edith. He shrugged, not really wanting to see either of them. He must be getting desperate, though, standing in a phone booth watching the girls go by, fantasizing. He focused on the telephone booth where a spider was adding to a complex network of cobwebs above the telephone.

The Seattle number rang through to an answering service. Closed until Monday. Damn Charlotte and her trail of chaos!

He strode down the ramp, hurried out the float toward *Misfit*, Charlotte's rather appropriately named boat. His mind was back in Vancouver, dealing with the land option and the contractors' bids for the North Shore development.

As he turned onto the last finger, he caught one glimpse of that warm confusion of curly hair. The woman with the bundle. His heart crashed against his rib cage in a wild beat before he pushed the crazy fantasy out of his mind.

If he was stuck here overnight, perhaps she would be free for the evening. He felt a heavy pulse beating through his body. Crazy! She wasn't beautiful, just ... something.

He passed a big white powerboat, then a two-masted blue schooner—at least, he thought it was a schooner. His eyes raked over the boats. Had she gone inside one of them? Which one? The white? The blue? Why the hell did it matter? Was she inside that old wooden monstrosity at the end, just opposite Charlotte's?''

Then he saw her, standing in the cockpit of *Misfit* with a mass of blue material spread out in front of her. He jerked to a stop, staring at her.

"What the hell are you doing here?" He heard the echo of his own voice and wondered where the anger came from, and why it bothered him to find she had some connection with his sister.

"Who are you?" That was better. His voice was quiet now. He strode along the little float, stopped when he was close enough to see that her eyes were wide and green and staring. He gripped the stanchion but did not step up onto the boat, mainly because he could feel his heart thudding and felt an insane urge to touch her face, feel the softness of those shining curls. A total stranger! What was the matter with him? Delayed adolescence! He cleared his throat.

The silence was alive. She turned away. As she moved, he could see that she was fitting the blue fabric onto the shining metal tubing over the hatch. The clothes she was wearing were not cotton, but natural canvas. Deceptively simple, the kind of garments that turned out to cost four times what you expected. The shirt seemed shapeless, with green trim at neck and wrists to echo the color of her eyes. Shapeless, but it hung on her in some magical way that hinted at the woman's curves underneath.

"What are you doing here?" he demanded.

"Fitting the dodger on." Her voice was slightly husky. She had laughed with the workman up at the road, but she was not smiling now. She was frowning, although she had faint lines around her mouth that told him she laughed easily.

That hair, all coppery wildness. The life in the way she moved. He didn't know just what it was, but she bothered him. And he wanted her.

Her eyes were locked on the dodger as she did something to a zipper and muttered, "You're Kent Ferguson, aren't you?"

CHAPTER TWO

ANGELA would have recognized him anywhere. She might have known him even if Charlotte had not shown her the picture, just from the description and the deep blue of his eyes. Eyes like Charlotte's. Thirty-five, Charlotte had said, but he looked older when he frowned.

He was cold and controlled, according to Charlotte, but a minute ago he had been shouting—at her. Angela didn't like being shouted at. She concentrated on the zipper, pulling it closed so that the dodger stretched tightly along the stainless steel bow of the frame.

He seemed taller than the six feet Charlotte had said he was. He was wearing a dark suit with the jacket open, and a subdued tie that shrieked quiet class. Too hot, she would have thought, but he looked cool all the way from his dark blond hair right down to the black city shoes.

He would be very good-looking if he smiled, but he was frowning and she did not suppose he would tell her anything, although she asked anyway.

"Do you know where Charlotte is?"

His frown grew deeper. "How did you know I was her brother?"

Who else would turn up on the marina floats dressed for high finance and the big city? She smothered a smile and said truthfully enough, "Family resemblance."

"You're dreaming."

His dry disbelief was an insult to Charlotte, and Angela felt like smacking him, slamming the red imprint of her hand on to his tightly drawn cheek. She gave the zipper a hard, angry tug, knowing that hitting him would be pointless.

"Did Charlotte send for you?" If she had, it wasn't good news for Harvey. Angela bit her lip. "Is that why you're here?"

"You could say that. What are *you* doing there? What's that blue thing?"

"It's a dodger—protection from the rain. Charlotte ordered it." She moved around to the front of the plastic windshield and snapped it down to pull it tight. The dodger was a perfect fit, taut and smooth. It fitted on to the boat as if it belonged, the blue fabric a perfect match for Charlotte's sail covers.

"But it covers only the hatch." The frown was in his voice. "Not much use for someone standing in the cockpit."

Angela looked across at him, her eyes suddenly filled with laughter. "Have you never been sailing in the rain?"

"I've never been sailing, period."

"Too much time behind a desk," she speculated. "You're missing a whole world." She took a piece of chalk out of her pocket and marked where she would sew a reinforced slot for the mainsheet. Give him just one week of summer sailing and that wavy hair would change from brownish to a streaky, heart-stopping blond. He might learn to smile, too.

She rubbed out part of the chalk line and drew it back slightly to the right. "Sailing to windward in the rain, this dodger will keep most of the misery off. As for the hatch, without the dodger, every time you slide it open when it's raining the water on top of it ends up down inside."

"I'll take your word for it." His wry voice made her realize that she probably sounded as if she were lecturing her six-year-old nephew.

She felt the motion of the boat when he stepped on to it. Her eyes jerked up. The man was too much, dressed as if he owned the world and looking like it too, with those shoulders and that harsh, thin face. She had an urge to see him in something less formal than a suit, wondered if a canvas fisherman's shirt and blue jeans would make him less intimidating.

"Did you actually make that?" He had his hand on the edge of the dodger, his eyes narrowed as he studied the intricacy of its structure.

"Yes," she agreed. "I'm the dodger lady." Silly thing to say. She shrugged, then added, "I do quite a business in sailboat dodgers. Are you in the market?"

She looked and found his eyes on her, the coolness gone and a disconcerting probing in its place.

He said something just as an engine started up on the boat beside *Misfit*. She blinked, re-focusing. "What did you say?" On Charlotte, those blue eyes flashed with emotion. His were cool again now, almost cold. She must have dreamed the emotion in them.

"I said, 'how much?'"

"How much what?"

He couldn't possibly mean what she thought. She had said "in the market," and he had asked "how much?" As if he were asking her price. She felt the heat crawling up her neck, knew her sensitive skin would be flushing and was almost certain he would notice. She must have imagined that heated question in his eyes a moment ago, she must be completely off balance this morning. Or maybe it was just chemistry that was making her feel awkward, unexpectedly and uncomfortably aware of his tall, lean masculinity.

"Money. Dollars. How much does my sister owe you for your work?"

"Oh, that. Ah——" She shoved her hand through her hair.

He reached into the breast pocket of his jacket and pulled out a leather folder. His checkbook. A pen. A fountain pen, of course, and that was probably real gold.

She muttered, "Charlotte will pay me."

Abruptly, tension flared between them. "*I'll* pay you." His blue eyes glared ice at her.

Angela demanded, "Where is she?" not intending to shout, but finding her voice loud and aggressive.

"God knows," he muttered, and she wondered suddenly if those harsh lines leading down his cheeks concealed anger, or some other emotion.

"Don't you even *care* where she is?"

"Not particularly." His eyes raked over her. She felt as if he knew exactly what she would look like without the shirt, without the pants. She felt . . . invaded . . . off balance, then angry as he snapped, "I'm in a hurry. Just tell me how much, leave the blue stuff, and clear out."

She had not expected to dislike him, had never thought she would meet him. There weren't many people she actively disliked. She shook her hair back. His lips were thinned in irritation. There was no anger now, just impatience.

She snapped, "You just show up and figure you're going to turn everything upside-down, take over Charlotte's affairs and——"

"Not that it's any of your business, but I'm here because she asked." He lifted cold blue eyes from the checkbook.

"But Charlotte——"

"Is gone. On to the next adventure." He sounded bored.

"Oh, no!" she whispered. Poor Harvey. Poor Charlotte, falling in love and afraid to trust it, running away because she was afraid to explain to Harvey. "But the boat was open," she protested weakly. "Charlotte must have come back and——"

"I opened it." He was writing something on the check. The date. "What's the name of your business? And how much?"

Angela gripped the fabric. "Harvey said that the moorage is only paid until Sunday, so she'll be back."

He straightened, and she felt fear. Crazy, because he was just a man, very civilized, and they were in the middle of a busy marina. But when he snapped, "Who's Harvey?" she jumped.

"My—they—they're in love." He would not understand about love, about caring. Not with those eyes. "Listen, Mr. Ferguson, you can put away your pen. Charlotte will be back by Sunday. She's just gone away to think for a bit, and——"

"Charlotte doesn't think. She simply reacts."

Angela gritted her teeth and ground out, "You, on the other hand, don't feel. You just think."

A speedboat passed behind them, setting up a wake and rocking *Misfit*. Kent reached out and grasped a shroud overhead, holding himself against the motion. "Do you want to get paid or not?"

She bit her lip. Harvey was so sure Charlotte would be back. "How do I know you're telling the truth?"

He sighed. "Lady, I'm trying to pay you some money. I'm the messenger boy, here to tidy up my big sister's loose ends, and you're a loose end. But if you want documentary evidence—does this constitute proof?"

"This" was a telegram. Angela let go of the fabric and took it from his hand, felt a jolt of sensation as his fingers brushed hers. She yanked her hand away and concentrated on the telegram. "You're taking away the boat? She's in Seattle? Where? Which hotel is she in?"

He shrugged indifferently. "She sent the telegram from Seattle. She's probably in Hong Kong by now. Or Paris. Who knows?"

"You *must* know!" If he cared, he would know. She was not sure that he cared. Oh, Lord! Poor confused Charlotte. That weekend, over in Mystery Bay, Charlotte had talked and Angela had listened, but there hadn't seemed much to say except, "Why don't you tell Harvey? I'm sure he'd be understanding."

Charlotte had run away, so that must have been the wrong thing to say. What if Charlotte was gone because Angela had said "tell Harvey" and that was simply impossible?

Kent Ferguson, here because Charlotte had sent for him. That was ironic in a horrible way. He was frowning, announcing cynically, "I'll know where she is when the bills come in. If you don't want a check now, send me the bill." He slipped something out of the leather case and she found a business card in her fingers.

She wanted to crumple it in her hand. "You can't just write a bunch of checks and walk away. You——"

"Can't I?" His lips twitched. "A suitable check looks after most problems, I've found."

"If I'm one of those problems, you won't get rid of me with a check." She pushed the card into her pocket. "You're taking the boat away now?" This boat was Harvey's only real link with Charlotte. "Where——? No, you can't! I've got alterations to do to the dodger first. You have to leave the boat here until——"

"The dodger will do as it is."

"No! It needs—this is just the first fitting. I can't leave it like this. It's not finished, not right."

"Oh, for——" She jerked back as he towered over the cockpit. His eyes were suddenly hot. Something flashed between them, leaving her breathless. She pressed against the side of the cockpit, away from him, and pressed her lips tightly together to keep the yelp of panic inside.

"I'm not about to assault you." His eyelids had dropped until his eyes were only slits in his harsh face. "Excuse me, but I want to go inside for my briefcase."

He brushed her arm as he swung through the companionway. She felt the fleeting touch as an angry jolt right through her body. He was gone only a second, reappearing with a leather attaché case. She had not moved while he was gone, but she wished she had. The cockpit seemed so small, too small.

He stopped, staring down at her. He was not quite as tall as he had seemed, but the shoulders made him seem massive. He must have his suits tailored especially for those shoulders. He smiled, but there was no softness, no friendliness in the twist of his lips.

"I admit that the thought of ravishing you had occurred to me, but that was before you opened your mouth." She gasped and he seemed to tower even more threateningly. "The appeal wore off quite quickly," he murmured. "You're almost as much trouble as my sister."

She swallowed. The man had a physical impact like a steamroller. He frightened her, but she couldn't just let him sail away, for Harvey's sake.

She muttered, "Charlotte's in love with Harvey—I'm sure she is. She just—they just—if he could see her, talk to her——"

He put the briefcase on top of the hatch, snapped it open and took out his cellular telephone. "Charlotte's been in love so many times, it's nothing new or special. When it's over, she leaves me to clean up the mess."

"You're the problem, not the solution."

He stared at her. "What the hell do you mean by that?"

She gasped, "Nothing. I—— Don't you——?"

He punched three numbers on the telephone, stopped and demanded, "Don't I what?"

"Don't you wonder why Charlotte sent you a telegram instead of telephoning? I'd avoid talking to you,
too. You're a hard man, and you don't give a damn about
anyone, do you?"

He caught her arm, his hand closing around her wrist.
She jerked, pulling his fingers painfully tight. He lifted
her hand, holding her against him for a moment before
she tore away. There was so little room, just this tiny
cockpit and a man who seemed to radiate virility. She
felt an unwilling tightness at the pit of her stomach as
her eyes were trapped by his.

She thought she heard a ringing sound, then realized
it was in her head, some spell he had her under. He
seemed frozen, his fingers curled around her wrist, his
eyes digging into her soul.

"What do you want?" she breathed. "For just an in-
stant she thought that he wanted *her*.

She twisted her hand and the sun caught the gold of
her wedding ring. Then suddenly she was free, falling
back against the cockpit seat, stumbling and sitting down
with a thud.

She jerked back to her feet. "If you ever touch me
again, I'll——" She shook her head, heard her own
breath heavy and ragged. "Let me out of here."

She stumbled past him, jumped onto the float and
heard him moving behind her. She had to get away before
she went right to pieces. The man made her feel vulnerable, shaken, as if she were a young girl. When he
had held her imprisoned with his fingers around her
wrist, his body hard and close to hers, she had felt the
most incredible urge to melt into him.

"What's your name, dodger lady?"

She did not answer, just kept moving. She hurried
along the float on to the main finger, not looking where
she was going until she cannoned straight into a big
woman pulling a carry-all cart.

"Sorry!" Angela was out of breath, as if she had been running. Maybe she was knocked a bit senseless too, because it took a second for her to realize who she had smashed into. Then she blinked and mumbled, "Theresa, I'm sorry. I wasn't looking."

Theresa, big and friendly and interested in everybody's business, smiled at her. "How's everything, Angie? Did you hear about the accident on Water Street? A taxi and a bus. They say Ernie Wenchen's boy was driving the cab, and he's being charged."

Angela felt like a fly trapped between two overwhelming forces. Theresa in front of her with an endless fountain of gossip; Kent Ferguson coming up behind her.

"Theresa, have you met Kent Ferguson? Charlotte's brother, you know." Theresa blinked and Angela thought she could feel the man's anger behind her. She added, "Charlotte from *Misfit*."

"Oh?" Theresa's prying eyes lit up, focusing on the man behind Angela. "Her brother? You're much younger, aren't you?"

Angela stepped aside and left him facing the formidable Theresa. If he got free in less than five minutes, he was even more forceful than she had thought. She could hear his voice as she walked away. He sounded politely bored, and she almost laughed. Training, she thought. A man who dressed like that, moved like that, would have been well trained in all the social graces. He wouldn't be rude, except in the most well-mannered fashion.

Yet a moment ago he had grabbed her like a forceful, impulsive caveman. Her heart crashed against her ribs as she remembered his fingers holding her, his hard chest against her breasts. His eyes—— No, he hadn't really intended to do that, to seize her and pull her close for that breathless moment. It had been madness for him too. By the time he got free of Theresa he would have lost the urge to chase after her.

She went up the ramp to her van, opened the door and slid in. It was stuffy inside, the sun beating through the windshield. She opened the window and cranked the key, pumping the throttle hard to start the temperamental engine.

She saw him coming up the ramp, not hurrying. He walked deliberately between the van and the small car beside it. He put one hand on her door, his fingers inside, only an inch away from her shoulder. She felt her heart give an erratic, disturbed thud.

"What's your name?" he demanded.

His voice had lost the anger now. He sounded indifferent.

She shrugged. "Angela Dalton." There was no reason not to tell him.

"Dalton?" He looked down at her hand on the steering wheel. "Is that your married name?"

She stared at her own hands. The wedding ring. Time you took it off, Barney had said more than once. She was glad she hadn't, because crazy though it seemed, she wanted barriers, walls, to protect her from this stranger.

She curled her fingers more tightly around the steering wheel. "Yes. That's my married name."

"Where's your husband?"

He was a man who always got his way. She turned her head and tried to see in his eyes what he wanted. What had he said back there on the boat? That he had thought about ravishing her? She gulped and jerked her eyes away from him. Where was her usual cool mask, her ability to radiate "no" without words?

"Where is he?" he repeated.

"Do you want to meet him?" She pushed her foot down to make the engine roar. He jerked, as if he thought she might shove the van into gear and take his hand off. Her husband. Barney was right, she should have taken Ben's ring off years ago. She shook off her natural tendency to tell the truth and said on a rush, "Come to the shop and I'll introduce you to him."

She twisted to look through the back window of the van as she shifted into reverse. Damn! There was the bow of a sailboat just coming into view on the road behind. Why did they have to drive the Travelift past right now? A big blue framework on wheels, the Travelift picked boats out of the water, hung them from slings attached to the blue arms, and slowly, so slowly, moved the boats around the waterfront area. Usually the boats were moved from the water to the shipyard, but sometimes they crawled along the road, the big Travelift tires crunching slowly, taking the boats elsewhere. Right now two boats were parked outside Dalton Welding and Canvas, blocked up to be worked on by Barney and his welder.

Angela bit her lip and watched the slow progress of the lift and boat through her back window. She could feel the man beside her, stole a glance and was relieved to find that he had straightened up to watch. He wasn't touching her van.

There were no other vehicles around, no hand on her door to stop her. She reversed and turned, just clearing the wheels of the lift. He was watching her. Or was he watching the lift? She forced herself not to look, concentrating on the yellow sailboat in the lift, the mossy stuff hanging down from the underwater hull, still dripping. When there was room, she pushed the van into forward gear and drove slowly between the crawling lift and the line of parked cars.

He had told her to leave the dodger as it was, and although she'd marked the alterations that would allow the sail handling lines to pass through, she had left without taking the dodger. If she went back tomorrow, the boat would probably be gone, and the job not properly finished.

All right, he had won that round. Angela was a perfectionist in her work, but she didn't think she was prepared to face Kent Ferguson again. Okay, but she was darned if she would send a bill! The deposit Charlotte had paid would cover the materials, so she was just minus her labor costs and Barney's to make the stainless steel bows. She'd talk to Barney, and he would go along with her. No invoice, and Charlotte might some day realize that the dodger was not paid for. That would bother her, might even bring her back.

Harvey was not at the shop when Angela got there. She dialed the house and when he answered she blurted, "Dad, there's a man down at Charlotte's boat. He's her—her brother." Oh, God! Charlotte's big secret, and she had almost blurted it out as if it were common knowledge. She added quickly, "He's come to take the boat. She sent him a telegram, asked him to come down here and clear up everything, take the boat back to Vancouver."

Harvey was speechless for a moment, then he said decisively, "I'm going down there to talk to him."

She wished she could make herself go too, a buffer between Harvey and Kent Ferguson, but she did not want to see that man again, so she started laying out red Sunbrella on her cutting table, preparing for cutting sail covers. She would be ahead of schedule on the covers because she had scheduled today for Charlotte's final adjustments.

She jerked when she heard the bell that signaled the door opening, but when she looked up it was only Barney's wife Sally with Jake.

"Barney here?" Sally was short and roundish and pretty, with blonde fly-away hair and an absentminded smile that Barney had fallen for when he was only eighteen. She had her son's little hand firmly in hers, her other hand resting on the round swelling of late pregnancy. Jake tugged, wanting freedom, but Sally looked around first, searching for trouble her six-year-old son might get into.

"Barney's welding in the shop," warned Angela. "So best leave Jake here with me while you go in. Coffee's on," she added, jerking her head toward the coffeepot in the corner.

Free, Jake made straight for the cutting table, his small hands curling around its edge. "Can I help, Aunt Angie? I like red." His straight blond hair was almost white, topping a thin, serious face that held startling, wide brown eyes.

She looked around quickly, knowing Jake was best kept occupied. "Why don't you roll up that red binding tape? Over there on the rack." The binding was streaming off the roll because Angela had been measuring it, but better to have Jake rolling it back up than grabbing the fabric she was cutting.

Sally, seeming shorter than usual with her body rounded by pregnancy, waddled over to the coffeepot and looked at it, decided, "No, I'd better not. When I've had this little hellion, I'm going to drink five gallons of coffee."

"You'll be nursing," Angela reminded her with a smile. "How about some herb tea? Why don't you plug in the kettle, and I'll join you in a minute? What did the doctor say?"

Her sister-in-law grimaced. "Two weeks more, and too bad if I'm dying in the heat." Sally shook her head, her pale blue eyes rueful. "The man had the nerve to say it wasn't a very hot summer, that it was *my* body thermostat gone haywire." She placed both hands on her swollen stomach and muttered, "Why didn't Barney and I time this better? It was the same with Jake. Far better to be pregnant in the winter, you know. The warmth comes in handy."

Angela smiled, knowing that Sally and Barney had been trying for a second baby ever since Jake's birth, that summer or winter made no difference to either of them.

When Sally went into the shop to find Barney, Angela concentrated on the sail covers, cutting the long pieces with one eye on Jake.

"I want to sew," announced Jake when he had the binding coiled up.

"Okay. How about red?"

His eyes lit up. "Can I make a sail cover? Like you do?"

She set up the red thread on the lightweight machine, then gave Jake two long scraps of cuttings from the floor. He had known how to use the machine for almost a year, and although he sewed in ragged circles, he didn't often get her thread snarled up, so she didn't mind. She liked working with her nephew around.

If her baby had lived...

She pushed that thought away. It was pointless to cry for what was gone. She folded the two long pieces for the mains'l cover and started laying out for the matching jib bag.

The door crashed open again and the uniformed UPS man hurried in. She signed for two rolls of fabric and three boxes, then gave him the box of canvas shirts she was shipping to a sporting goods shop in Seattle. If she got many more orders for the clothing line she was developing, she would have to find someone to help with the sewing.

She was cutting when the door opened again.

"Harvey, how——?"

She broke off, seeing the man behind Harvey, then heard the slick sound of her own scissors sliding through fabric. She looked down. Darn! She had cut straight into the piece. She would either have to throw it out and cut anew, or modify the bag to make the extra seam appear to belong.

Jake got up from the machine, pulling the red pieces out, and Angela said automatically, "Jake, honey, cut off the thread. It's still connected."

He bent his thin body over the task. "It's a cover for a baby sailboat," he announced to his grandfather. He put it down in front of Angela, on top of the ruined sail bag piece, and decided, "I want a red fisherman's shirt."

"Another one?" asked Harvey. He was smiling, although his face was strained and gray. Behind him, Kent Ferguson had stopped, his eyes taking in everything from the mess of cuttings on the floor around Angela's feet to Jake's sun-bleached mop of hair.

"Kent," Harvey said, his gesture inviting the stranger inside their shop, "this is my daughter-in-law, Angela. She runs this place, really. Estimates and canvas work, and scheduling for the rest of us."

"We've met," said Kent briefly. "Down at Charlotte's boat."

Angela swallowed, staring at him. What was it about the man that bothered her so much? He should be the one to look out of place, with his city suit and shining black shoes, hard blue eyes. Instead, he made her very aware of the disorganized chaos around her.

Jake pressed against her, staring at the stranger. Harvey added, "And my grandson, Jake. Jake's got a wardrobe of fishermen's shirts you wouldn't believe." Harvey made a gesture to a display rack near the door. "Angie's started this line of boating clothes—Sailing Rags, she calls them. They've become all the rage around here. She can hardly keep up with the demand."

Angela wished Harvey would stop talking. Why was Kent Ferguson here? If Harvey had invited him to stay up at the house, she was going to go somewhere else. A trip to Seattle, or anywhere. There was no way she could sleep if that man was under her roof!

"... if you guys can spare me," Harvey was saying.

"What?" Angela had missed something. All she could see was Kent's eyes, laughing because he knew somehow that she didn't have her mind on what was happening. "What did you say, Dad?"

"I said I'd take Charlotte's boat up to Vancouver. Kent needs someone to deliver it, and I could use a couple of days off. I'll leave on Sunday, should be back by Tuesday."

"Oh." She knew why he was doing it. Taking Charlotte's boat would be a link with the woman he loved. Had he talked to Kent about the relationship between himself and Charlotte? She realized both men were staring at her and said quickly, "I'll reschedule the welding on the tugboat."

"Or get Barney to do it," suggested Harvey, adding to Kent, "Barney's my son. Good boy. Not a boy now, of course. He's pretty well taken over the welding and engineering from me. I just do a bit to keep my hand in."

"I'm going to be a welder," announced Jake suddenly. His voice was so quiet that Angela thought no one had heard but her.

"Like your father?" asked Kent. The man must have incredible hearing.

"Yeah," agreed Jake, clutching the tiny boat sail cover to his chest, staring at Kent. "Like my dad."

Angela wished Kent would stop watching her. He was talking to Jake, then reaching for his checkbook to give Harvey a check to cover expenses getting the boat up north. Harvey shook his head and Angela thought it must hurt him to think about taking money to do something for Charlotte.

"Forget it," said Harvey. "That's far too much. It's only going to cost the fuel to fill up *Misfit*'s tanks. I don't want anything for my time. I haven't been sailing in a long time, it'll be a pleasure."

She gathered the fabric together and announced, "I'm going upstairs to stitch this." She had another commercial machine up there, the one she normally used for doing the zig-zag over-stitch on sail covers and dodgers.

"Me too," announced Jake, following her up the stairs.

Upstairs, she dropped the fabric onto the big sewing table and stared at it until Jake urged her, "Aunt Angie, aren't you going to sew? You said you were going to sew."

"Yeah." She was sorry about Charlotte, for Harvey's sake, but it would be an incredible relief when that man walked out of Dalton Welding and Canvas. Once *Misfit* was gone, there was no reason Kent Ferguson would ever have to come back to Port Townsend.

"Who is he?" asked Jake, as if he were following her thoughts.

"He's Charlotte's brother." She added, "And I don't like him."

Jake sat on a roll of canvas, propping his elbow on his knee and dropping his chin into his palm. "Why don'cha like him?"

"I don't know." He made her feel flustered, too aware of him as a man. It was years since she had felt like that. She picked up the red Sunbrella and started to smooth it, matching the pieces that would be sewn together. "Because he watches me all the time," she decided. She knew she was overreacting, but it was an instinctive response, something chemical. Kent Ferguson was trouble, and she certainly didn't need trouble in her life. Not ever again.

"I don't like him either," announced Jake loyally.

Harvey's boots trooped up the stairs a few minutes later.

"Is he gone?" asked Angela.

"Hmm. Gone to the airport. He's got a jet there, waiting to take him back to Vancouver."

"He would." It fitted the clothes. Money, but of course there had to be money somewhere to pay for the way Charlotte wandered around at will.

Harvey sank down beside Jake. "He doesn't know where Charlotte is." His brown eyes filled with worry. "I've just got to believe that she'll come back some time. I really don't know how to start looking for her."

Only three years ago Harvey had lost Anna, and they had all thought he would never smile again. Then Charlotte had come breezing into port, the fifty-one-year-old bombshell with her laughter and her easy warmth. Harvey had started to smile again, to laugh. Then he had asked Charlotte to marry him.

"Marriage," Charlotte had confessed to Angela out on Mystery Bay. "It scares the hell out of me. I almost tried it twice, Angie, but—I just couldn't do it. Not when it came down to the wire. What if—what if I got myself tied to a jerk? What if——?"

"Harvey's not a jerk," Angela had said that day.

"No. Oh, no, he's not! But I'm a coward, I always was. I—if a relationship's going to work, it's got to be founded on truth, hasn't it?"

Angela had nodded, although she was no expert. She had seen love, happiness, but it had always been other people. Barney and Sally. Harvey and Anna. Her own love, the one time she tried, had turned to ashes.

So Charlotte had run away, because she could not bring herself to share the truth with Harvey, and now Harvey said, "I wish I knew why she felt she had to run away."

Angela bit her lip. Should she tell him why? "What about her brother?" She could not bring herself to say his name. Kent. Her mind whispered it, which frightened her because she could feel his eyes on her, the way he had stared the whole time she was downstairs. "Couldn't he find her, if he wanted to?"

Harvey sighed. "Maybe. He doesn't know where she is now, but it's a contact anyway. We've got his address, and I'm going to leave a letter for Charlotte on the boat, in case she comes back to it. And I'll leave a letter with him, too, for her. Where the devil can she be, Angie? Where's she gone?"

"Can I come?" Jake asked suddenly. He was assembling scraps on the floor, putting them together as if they were a jigsaw puzzle. "Grandpa, can I came sailing with you? My dad says I'm a good sailor. I'll work hard."

CHAPTER THREE

On August the first Kent flew to Vancouver Island to meet the architect he'd retained for the new development. He returned to Vancouver in time to go over the specifications on the North Shore job with the contractor. Then he flew to Ottawa, where he sweltered through two humid days of meetings with a government committee on urban renewal.

Charlotte's telegram came while he was in Ottawa. "I'm at the San Francisco Sheraton. Please forward mail. Charlotte." By the time Kent got back to the office, Patricia had already forwarded the mail.

Kent would have expected Charlotte to turn up farther away. When she left the lawyer from New York, she had surfaced in Tokyo. After that affair with the Mexican two years ago, she'd run to Cyprus. San Francisco was close enough that she might not be sure she should be running. Was Angela right? Did Charlotte love Harvey Dalton?

Trying to second-guess his sister was impossible. Love? What the hell did the word mean, anyway? Did it mean Charlotte in another mess?

Kent picked up the telephone to call his accountant and somehow ended up dialing his pilot instead, ordering the Lear made ready for another flight to Port Townsend. Harvey Dalton was the steadiest thing that had turned up in Charlotte's life in a long time. Maybe he was just what Charlotte needed.

He knew his actions weren't making a lot of sense. He never interfered in Charlotte's life, just paid the bills and arranged to have the scattered pieces picked up. There was nothing different this time…only the woman who had been haunting his dreams. Strangely erotic dreams for a man who didn't have time for relationships—especially with married women.

That was stupid, asking for trouble, but if it wasn't Angela Dalton drawing him back to Port Townsend, why didn't he simply call Harvey Dalton on the telephone and pass on Charlotte's address?

A married woman, with a child. Yet he had to go back, perhaps needed to see her with the man she had married. To see—what? Her eyes lit with love for another man? That might be just the thing to kill this ridiculous haunting. He had woken in a heated sweat too many times in the last three weeks, alone in his apartment. Last week he had called Sheila and taken her to dinner, then back to his apartment, but the dreams hadn't stopped.

Thirty-five. Wasn't that the age for some kind of crisis in a man's life? Insanity, he suspected, because there was no reason for it. He knew almost nothing about her. She had wild, soft hair and hot green eyes. She sewed things and she did not like to leave a job unfinished. She did not hesitate to speak her mind. She walked as if she did not know what the swing of her hips did to a man. She wore a wedding ring.

Her eyes turned tender when she looked at the boy.

It would make as much sense for him to be obsessed by a picture of a woman in a magazine. If he wanted an affair, why not pick a woman closer, in Vancouver or on the North Shore? A woman without a husband. A woman who was interested, because even if he wanted her Angela Dalton was the kind of woman who would be loyal to her husband forever. And, damn it, he was *not* a man who went after other men's wives! Never!

At the Port Townsend airport, he found that the rental car Patricia had ordered was not available. He took a taxi to the agency and even there had to wait another thirty minutes for a car. He spent the time going over the pro forma statements his accountant had delivered to the office earlier. When he finally got the car, it was the Chevette again. Next time he would drive down, bring the Chrysler and...

Next time?

Dalton Welding and Canvas was in the midst of a chaotic flurry of activity. The giant framework of one of those motorized boat-lifting devices loomed outside the front door. There was no way he could get through the press of people and machinery, so Kent sat in the car and watched.

The Travelift drove up to the boat, its blue arms sliding along either side. Three men worked with the straps that hung from those big arms, slipping them under the green sailboat that was blocked up just outside the door.

Once the slings were in place, the Travelift's motor roared and the slings came tight under the belly of the sailboat, taking its weight. Then the men pulled the wooden blocks away from under the boat and Kent got out of the rental car.

The man standing under the bow of the boat looked like a younger edition of Harvey Dalton—brown hair, thick arms and muscular shoulders, brown eyes when he turned to stare at Kent. Perhaps thirty years old.

My son Barney, Harvey had said. A good boy. So this was her husband. Kent remembered the feel of her wrist under his grasp, the sharp desire he had felt to have her in his arms, at the mercy of his touch, his lips, his body. He remembered, too, the sick feeling in his gut when he saw that gold band around her finger.

Barney moved toward Kent, smiling wryly at all the chaos around him. "This'll be clear in five minutes. What can I do for you?'' His eyes took in Kent's suit and he asked, ''Have you come about the lease?''

''No. I'm looking for Harvey Dalton. Is he around?''

Barney pointed to a door halfway along the building. ''He's in the shop, welding.''

Kent felt a bad taste in his mouth. No point in pretending. He had come for Angela, but staring at Barney he knew it was impossible. He felt guilty, as if the betrayal had been real, not fantasized in dreams.

Jake was sitting on the floor with Angela's oldest scissors in his hands, cutting up a storm with her scraps.

''Aunt Angie, how long do mothers stay in the hospital?''

''A few days,'' answered Angela absently. She was sewing an order for a dozen fishermen's shirts. Three smalls. Six mediums. Three larges. Assorted colors of trim.

Jake snipped his way through a small piece of green Herculite. ''Are babies always so small?''

''Always,'' she agreed, grinning as she stretched the red trim along the neckline and snapped the pressure foot down.

''But our new baby's got no hair. She's not supposed to be bald.''

Angela tried not to laugh. ''Don't worry, the hair will come.'' She pressed the foot pedal. The surger hummed and performed its complex stitch.

The noise from the shop flowed in briefly as someone opened the connecting door. Angela glanced back, but it was only Harvey, not a customer. She pushed the foot lever to raise the pressure foot, pulled the fabric around and lined up the last of the red trim, then lowered the foot again.

Jake probed curiously, ''My daddy says it takes a mummy and a daddy to make a baby.''

"That's right," she agreed absently.

"So why didn't you and Uncle Ben have babies too?"

"Jake!" Harvey's voice snapped across the shop.

Angela bit her lip and stared at the fabric.

Jake frowned. "Was it because Uncle Ben died that you didn't have babies? Because there wasn't time?"

Angela could hear Harvey's indrawn breath behind her, although it didn't sound like Harvey at all.

Jake stared up at Harvey with his brown eyes widening. Uneasy, Angela twisted around just as Jake asked, "You're the man my aunt Angie doesn't like, aren't you?"

Oh, Lord! Kent Ferguson. Why had he come back? She stared at him, saw his blue eyes glaring back at her. She got up abruptly, leaving the shirt in the sewing machine.

"Hello." She gulped and focused on Harvey, Jake's words echoing in her ears. "I'm going to see if Barney's ready to come down and help me with that estimate."

She grabbed the canvas bag that held her measuring tape and notebook, rushed toward the shop door, avoiding those accusing blue eyes. Damn! She didn't have to like the man, did she? He didn't move out of her way. She swerved, dodged around Harvey and yanked open the door, muttering, "Dad, you'll stick around and keep an eye on Jake and the phone while we're gone?"

The telephone rang just as Angela got through the door. She kept going. Harvey would have to get it. There was no way she was going back into that shop while *he* was there. She spotted Barney just disappearing through the workshop door.

"Hey, Barney! I need you to come down to that power boat."

"The guy from Alaska? I——"

"Barney! We told him today!" She rammed her hands into the pockets of her pants.

He grimaced and grumbled, "Well, okay, but give me an hour to——"

"Barney!" She did not want to go back inside. "Barney, that man's inside—Charlotte's brother. I—I really don't want to be around. I—I don't like him." As Jake had so bluntly announced! "If we go now, he'll be gone by the time we're back."

Barney sighed. "What does he want?"

"I don't know. I don't care. Just come, would you? Please!"

They spent an hour with the Alaskan couple, Angela making notes of the skipper's complex requirements while Barney figured out the structural problem. Barney would make the stainless steel bows to support the fabric walls and plastic windows Angela would sew. They worked together on estimates, often arguing with each other about what was best. Usually the outcome of their arguments was a tight, attractive canopy or dodger. In this case, the customer wanted a complete canvas enclosure for his flying bridge, but he wanted so many openings in it that Barney had to protest.

"You can't have everything open like that, not unless you're willing to have me put an extra bow here."

Angela added, "You see, if everything opens, there's nothing left to hold the fabric tight when you open up."

"But we need a window back there." The skipper, a big muscular man, had a habit of dropping his hand on to his tiny wife's neck, his fingers curved around to collar her. The gesture irritated Angela, although the wife seemed as indifferent to it as she was to the enclosure they were discussing.

Angela suggested, "You can have a window without it actually opening," and they finally worked out a plan for the enclosure that was agreeable to everyone. Angela glanced at her watch. It was almost time for the shop to close. If they were delayed a few more minutes, she could go straight home, avoiding Kent Ferguson.

He wouldn't be there anyway. He would be gone, back to his empire in Canada. Good, she told herself, forcing her mind on to the big Alaskan skipper and his tiny wife. She did not care why he had come, so long as he was gone.

"Look," she suggested, "why don't we take a walk around the docks? I'll show you a Sunbrella dodger. It's about four years old. You'll see how well it stands up."

Barney shifted restlessly. "You do that with them, Angie, and I'll go on up to the hospital to visit Sally."

They walked around the floats, Angela leading the way, the skipper guiding his wife with that hand around the back of her neck. By the time they had looked at several different boats, it was after six.

Barney had taken his truck, so Angela walked back to the shop, stopping as she turned the corner, making sure the Chevette was gone. It was, and the van was still there, so Harvey hadn't left yet. They would drive back to the house, taking Jake with them. She'd make supper for the three of them, and by then she would have stopped feeling that imbalance that the Canadian man seemed to bring into her life. No wonder Charlotte had trouble dealing with him! Kent Ferguson was upsetting, just standing there staring at her he made her feel uneasy.

She got to the shop, but found it locked. Damn! Where had Harvey gone at this time of day, without the van? The workshop door was locked too. The whole place was dark, the "Closed" sign in the window, and the van sitting there. Harvey must have left it for her and gone home with Jake, perhaps catching a ride with a customer. The only problem was that *her* keys were locked inside with her driver's license and her wallet.

Barney up at the hospital, Harvey at home. She looked into the van, but he hadn't left the keys in the ignition. Oh, well, she would just have to walk.

She told herself the exercise was good for her, and after a few blocks she started feeling calmer. This *was* what she needed, walking alone, looking out over the waters of Puget Sound as she climbed the big hill up toward the post office.

A car pulled up beside her just as she was passing the old stone building that housed the post office.

"Angie! Hop in, I'll give you a ride."

It was Charles, the young chiropractor she had dated last year. He was smiling, pushing the door of his sports car open for her.

It would mean fending off a date with Charles, but her legs were starting to cramp after climbing that hill. She slipped into the leather seat, shut the door and felt the car moving smoothly away.

Charles glanced at her, then back at the road ahead as he turned left. "What have you been doing lately, Angie?"

"Not enough," she said wryly. "I'm wiped out, just climbing that hill. I'd better get more exercise."

"How about Sunday?" he offered. "We could hike along the beach to Point Wilson."

"I don't think so." She should have kept walking. Charles was good company, but what he wanted was marriage and a family.

Not that she wouldn't like that too. With the right man. But if she ever got married again, it would be to a man who wanted the same life-style she did, and Charles wasn't that man. He had ambitions to buy a practice in Seattle and she knew she was not a city girl, any more than she had been a wandering girl, which was what Ben had wanted.

She had loved Ben, a hot, tempestuous emotion that was too unsettling for her own good. She'd rushed into marriage, eloping when her parents refused their consent. Looking back, she knew her parents had been right to try to stop her. She had been too young, too naive to see Ben for the irresponsible and erratic person he had been.

In the beginning it had been all magic, Angela dreaming her dreams, not knowing they weren't Ben's dreams. Always moving, never staying long enough to put down roots. At first it was exciting, but she came to dread the next move, losing friends she hardly had time to make, always heading for the next construction job, the next town, from state to state across the country, living in a trailer that was the only permanence in their life.

Ben hadn't wanted a family. That had been Angela's dream. When she had finally become pregnant after five years of their footloose, wandering marriage, she had learned just how serious Ben was about not wanting to share his life with children.

She shivered, remembering that horrible day when she had found herself alone on the other side of the continent. Then she felt the blast of heat and realized that Charles had turned the heater on, making the sports car unbearably stuffy. He was talking, and she nodded, not wanting to tell him that she hadn't heard a word he said.

"I'll pick you up in half an hour, then, shall I?"

"What?" She'd better pay attention, or she'd end up married to Charles. She could have agreed to anything just now. He turned into her driveway and she protested, "I don't know if I feel up to going out tonight, Charles."

"You'd enjoy it." She had forgotten how his voice could be so gently persuasive. "You love the theater, and the play is supposed to be very funny. One of my patients was saying today that she and her husband went, and they laughed themselves silly.''

There was a red Chevette in the driveway.

Kent Ferguson.

Harvey was so openhanded, he'd probably invited him to stay the night. Oh, Lord! A whole evening of that man, staring at her. She hated the way he always seemed to be watching her. It made her nervous. And now, after Jake's outrageous statement that Angela didn't like him, it would be even worse.

Charles was still talking. She remembered now that his habit of gently talking until he got his own way was what had made her stop seeing him last year. She had been afraid that one day she might nod agreement at the wrong moment and end up married to Charles. Then she would spend the rest of her life in a three-bedroom apartment in Seattle, living with a very nice, slightly boring man.

But an evening with Kent Ferguson staring at her...

''All right,'' she agreed abruptly. ''Yes, Charles, I'll go to the play with you. An hour, you said? I'll be ready.''

She heard Kent Ferguson's voice as soon as she opened the door. It was almost the opposite of Charles's voice— forceful, determined. He didn't do a lot of gentle persuasion. He just rode roughshod over everyone else's wishes. She hung her canvas bag up in the hall cupboard and followed the voices. She might as well get this contact over with as soon as she could.

Jake was sitting in front of the television set with earphones on. Angela glanced at the screen and saw that he was playing the videotape of *Cinderella* again. He must have every line of dialogue memorized by now.

Kent was sitting in the big easy chair that Harvey usually took for himself. Harvey was sitting on the sofa across from him, and leaned forward, his face showing excitement. Just what was going on?

Kent was saying, "...at dawn. You should be there by nine. She's at the Sheraton Hotel."

Angela moved into the room. "Are you talking about Charlotte?"

Kent's body jerked, but he did not look at her. She hated the way he watched her all the time, but irrationally it bothered her now that he would not look at her.

Deliberately, she demanded, "How's Charlotte's boat?"

"Still floating." He shrugged. She wondered who did his laundry. The shirt he was wearing now was a subtle shade of off-white, the collar pressed to perfection. His hand was lying on his knee, the perfect pant crease sharp underneath his tapping finger.

"Where?" she persisted.

"Tied up at the Royal Vancouver Yacht Club."

"Sounds a bit stuffy for Charlotte." It suited him, though. Nothing but the best, the most expensive. His women would be expensive too, immaculate and polite and...willing.

Harvey said, "She's in San Francisco, Angie. Kent's going to take me down there in his plane in the morning."

"Does Charlotte know?" She could see from their faces that she didn't. "You're just going to burst in on her? Without warning?"

"I've got to talk to her, honey."

She nodded, knowing Harvey would not rest until Charlotte told him no to his face. But why was this man helping? As much as she liked Charlotte, Angela had had time to think since the older woman's disappearance. It was quite possible that Charlotte had done the best thing for both herself and Harvey, running away.

Harvey wanted to marry her, and Charlotte didn't think it would work. Angela wasn't sure it would work, either.

What really bothered her was why Kent Ferguson should go out of his way to be a matchmaker. It seemed totally out of character.

"Could you pack for me?" Harvey asked.

"Gladly. I'll do it now. By the way, Barney's gone to the hospital."

"I figured. Do you think he'll stay up there through dinner again?"

"Probably. He'll come and pick Jake up when he's done." Kent Ferguson was listening to every word, and she knew why. She could feel his awareness of her, could almost hear his voice telling her why he had really come into her house.

Because he had heard Jake's words, and he knew now that she was not married.

Harvey stood up and prowled to the window. "Kent's staying here for the night. I thought he could have the room across from yours."

Angela knew when Kent turned. She was not looking at him, but she felt his eyes on her face and knew she was flushing. The room across from yours.

"I'll make up the bed."

She turned away, glad of one more excuse to escape them. "And I'll pack your bag. The gray suit? You can wear the brown, and I'll pack the gray. You'll have to get supper for yourselves tonight, though. I'm going out with Charles."

"Charles?" Harvey had always liked Charles. He smiled and offered, "Look, Angie, you go ahead and get ready. I'll pack for myself."

"There's time." After she had made the bed and packed for Harvey, she would have just enough time to get ready. That was how she wanted it. She did not want to come back down here and sit trying to pretend she didn't feel uneasy.

She patted Jake's soft hair on her way past. He grunted, his eyes fixed on the screen where the wicked stepsisters were browbeating Cinderella. Angela went upstairs, got out sheets and made up the bed. This was the room Ben had used as a child, although there was nothing left of his personality here now.

Ben's childhood was preserved in pictures in Harvey's study, but the rest of the house had gone on living, closing up the empty space he had left behind. Poor Ben, erased as if he had never been. He had never been able to grow up, had abandoned Angela when marriage turned into responsibilities. In the end he had been alone on a freeway in Iowa, and it had been weeks before his family learned of the accident that had killed him.

Angela packed for Harvey, who normally wore a suit only to church. Then she ran herself a deep bath of hot water, drowning out the rumble of voices from downstairs. What on earth did they find to talk about? She had seldom seen two men less similar. Harvey with his work clothes and his weathered face, talking to a man who played games with money and property, who probably didn't even own a pair of jeans. If he owned running shoes, she thought, they would be immaculate and white, and the most expensive on the market.

Charlotte might have fitted into their lives like a breath of fresh air, but *he* was completely out of place.

Tomorrow he would be gone, flying Harvey to San Francisco. She hoped it would work out, that Charlotte wouldn't feel desperately cornered when Kent and Harvey turned up to confront her.

Kent. She did not want to think of him like that. Mr. Ferguson. She tried that out, but it didn't come very easily to her mind. Living on the edge of the water, dealing with sailors and fishermen, there weren't many times when she called anyone Mister. But it fitted him, fitted the kind of world he lived in, the high-class world of money and stilted manners.

Her parents' world. Not hers.

She soaked in the bath, trying to settle the crazy pounding of her heart. It must be because she knew Charlotte's secret that he made her feel so unsettled. He kept staring at her, and she was afraid that if she spent too much time around him Charlotte's secret might come out in an unwilling burst of words.

Angela didn't believe in keeping that kind of secret, but the truth was Charlotte's to tell. Not Angela Dalton's business at all, except that the other woman had confided in her.

Charles was five minutes early. He had changed from his daytime suit to more informal pants and the brown sweater she had once told him she liked. Angela wore a blue Mexican skirt that Charlotte had given her, with a matching blouse that laced together at the front. The skirt swirled around her as she popped her head into the living room. "Charles is here. I'm off now."

"Have a good time," said Harvey, smiling.

"I will." She made herself laugh, as if Charles stirred her blood and her heart. Kent Ferguson stood up, and her laughter died as he turned to face her. She would be so glad when he was gone.

His eyes narrowed. In this light his hair looked brown, not that disturbing blondish color. His eyes seemed more black than blue as he stared at her. "Good evening," he said, his words deliberate. "I'll see you later."

Not if she could help it.

As Charles had promised, the play was hilarious. It took a while, but she managed to lose herself in the crazy antics of the absentminded receptionist on the stage who was turning her boss's psychiatric practice upside-down.

Afterward, Charles held her hand as they walked back to his car. His voice was quiet, persuasive. "I've got a bottle of champagne back at my place, and a frozen chocolate cake."

Trust Charles to remember that she loved chocolate! "I don't think so," she said gently. Alone together in his apartment, Charles would put gentle music on. Charles being Charles, the wrestling match would be subtle, but in the end that was what it would come to.

"How about a drink, then?" he suggested. "That bar down on the waterfront?"

"How about a late supper somewhere?" she countered, because she had not eaten and it was too early to go back.

"My place, then."

"No, Charles. How about McDonald's?"

He shuddered and she laughed, then he took her to a small restaurant in an old Victorian mansion that had been turned into a guest house. After dinner, she agreed to the bar. There was music, and dancing, and although Charles would have liked to waltz, she would only dance to the wilder music, keeping out of his arms fairly successfully.

When they left the bar some time after midnight, he caught her in his arms at the car. "Angela," he murmured, bending to kiss her neck. "I've missed you so much these months apart."

"Charles——" Damn! This was stupid of her.

"Marry me," he whispered as he moved his lips against her neck.

"Stop it, Charles! You're tickling me! I don't want to get married."

"Then . . ." His hand moved suggestively.

She snapped, "I don't want that either. Charles—look, I just—we're friends, all right? Just friends."

It was not all right at all. She had spent three months last year trying to tell him she was not the woman for him, and it was all undone in one stupid evening. A high price to pay to avoid a man whose blue eyes kept watching her. Too high. She could have spent the evening in her room, reading. Alone.

She got Charles into the driver's seat and he finally agreed to take her home, but in her driveway she had to wriggle her way out of his arms to get out of the car. Luckily the gear shift hampered his attempts to persuade her into his arms.

"Find someone else, Charles."

"I've been dating my new receptionist," he said slowly.

"Good." Angela had a vague memory of a girl with dark, straight hair and a frowning face. "That's good. She's a lovely girl."

At least the house was dark, with only the light over the veranda stairs glowing to show her the way home. She went quietly up the stairs, opened the door and heard the quiet crunch of Charles's tires on the drive. Never again. She had forgotten just how exhausting Charles could be.

Everything was beautifully quiet. Barney must have come and picked up Jake hours ago. Angela moved through the entrance without turning on a light. The moonlight drifting in from the living room was enough.

Dark and quiet. All asleep. Upstairs, he would be lying in the bed across the hall from hers. She moved past the arch that led into the living room, along the wide corridor to the kitchen. There she opened the fridge and used the light inside it to find a glass. Ice and ginger ale. She sipped it, the bubbles tingling her nose.

She closed the fridge door and the darkness floated back in around her. She had left her shoes beside the front door, and was moving about in her nylon-covered feet, silently, almost a ghost in the big old house that must be filled with the spirits of the Victorian family who had built it.

Too big for just herself and Harvey, but it was the home of Harvey's happiness, the place where he had loved Anna until she died, where they had brought up their two sons. Anna's ghost was here, too, but Anna was a gentle woman and had been more of a mother to Angela than her own mother.

She went into the living room, making for the window where moonlight showed the hillside and the mountains across the water from Port Townsend. She could feel the ghosts around her, but it was a comfortable feeling, the knowledge that she was not really alone here despite the darkness and the sleeping house.

She almost dropped her glass when she heard the voice behind her.

CHAPTER FOUR

EVERYTHING in the room was shadows, black and gray shapes. Angela stared into the room, the moonlit sky at her back, and she finally made out Harvey's chair. A shadow, a man sitting there.

"Did you enjoy your reunion?" His voice was low in the darkness. His eyes would be hard, watching her, seeing only shadows.

She moved, realizing she was sharply silhouetted against the window. "What reunion?"

There was no movement, just his presence in the dark room, and his voice, accusing, "Harvey says you haven't been out with Charles in months. Why tonight?"

Her fingers curled tighter around the cool glass. She started to say something, anything, but changed her mind and her words, and spoke the truth.

"You know why. To avoid you."

He was between her and the archway to the corridor. She would go past him, upstairs, and shut herself in her room. But her legs would not move. What if he rose from that chair, swift and silent, his hand reaching out to stop her? What if he touched her?

Nervous, she whispered, "What does Charles matter to you? What do I matter?"

"Why did you tell me you were married?"

She felt the tightness in her chest. Behind her, a cloud must have passed over the moon. The world turned dense and dark.

"You let me think Barney was your husband."

She gulped—self-defense. He frightened her. "It's none of your business."

She heard some sound of fabric on fabric. He was getting up. She jerked into motion, her feet silent on the carpet. She had the advantage over him, knew the geography of this room intimately. She would escape him and——

She gasped and jerked to a halt. He had not touched her, but she could feel his presence, his body there, in front of her, just a denser darkness, not form. She was intensely aware of the darkness, the sleeping house, the size and presence of the man in front of her.

"Let me past." It should have been sharp, a demand, but her voice was only a breathless whisper.

"No."

She wanted to step back, to put space between them, but he seemed aware of every move she made, even in the darkness. She was afraid that, if she moved, he would reach out and catch her arms in his hands.

She shivered and hugged herself and asked, "What do you want?"

"You know what I want."

Could he hear her heart thudding wildly in the darkness? She knew what he wanted. It was true. Insane—impossible, but she knew as if she could see his eyes.

"I don't like you." She stepped back, heard his breathing and knew he had moved with her.

"So Jake says, but it's a lie."

She tried to deny his words. He was dangerous. Anything that made her feel like this was dangerous.

"Angela, I know damned well that you feel it too."

"No."

His voice was husky. "Yes. Why else lie about your husband? Why run away tonight with the rejected Charles?"

"I didn't want to be near you. I don't like you!" She gasped as his fingers brushed her arm and snapped, "Don't!"

She was even more nervous when he laughed, the sound low and compelling. What was he going to do? Why didn't she stop him? Why did she feel so helpless, trapped by his words and the feel of his presence, too close?

"I'll scream."

"No, you won't."

His fingers found the side of her face, spread gently over her cheek. She shivered and told her throat to open, but nothing happened except his low murmur.

"You want to know, don't you, Angela? Just as I want to know..."

"Know?" She could feel his breath. She was shivering, sharply aware that the sun was down and the night cool, the heat turned too low in this big old house. "Know what?"

"What it will be like when I touch you."

"No..."

His fingers traced the curve of her cheek, found the shell of her ear and explored lightly, slipping gently over the gold stud in her ear, threading through her hair.

"Stop it!" Her scalp contracted with sensation. "I don't want——"

The fingers of his other hand covered her lips, moving, tracing the shape. He was so close, not touching except for those fingers on her lips, her scalp, but she could feel how near his lips were to hers.

"Then run, Angela." His voice was low, almost hoarse. His fingers left her lips and she was trembling when his mouth covered hers. A fleeting caress, an exploration, and her lips were parted, her breath coming in short pulses that left her chest empty with each inhalation.

His hands slid along the sides of her neck, feeling the cord of muscle that jumped to his touch, tracing the shape of her throat. "Run, Angela. If you don't want my touch, then go now."

"I can't." Her whole body was trembling. Just his fingers learning the curves of her throat, her neck, her jaw, but she could feel the touch everywhere, a hard knot of tension growing inside her. She wanted to beg him to stop, to walk away, but could not even whisper.

"Neither can I go away." His hands slid up into her hair and his voice turned husky with emotion. "I knew your hair would be soft...so soft...fiery curls clinging to my touch."

His mouth sought hers again. She was so tense, her body shaking with the effort of fighting that wild urge to melt into his. He found her mouth open, inviting, and his tongue slipped inside to explore the tender underside of her lips, the warm darkness.

So tender. She had not expected gentleness from his lips, his hands. If he had grasped and tried to overpower her, she could have fought him. But this...

She had been hugging herself, for warmth, but he found her wrists with his fingers and unwrapped her arms. With her hands against his chest, she could feel the slow, hard beat of his heart under her palms.

"Come here," he urged. She stumbled as he led her.

She whispered, "Oh, no!" but his arms took her with him, down into that big chair of Harvey's. She struggled then, trying to get up, feeling how much more vulnerable she was now. Standing, with his touch gentle on her, all she had to do was step back, if she could *make* herself step back. But, here, she was sitting with his thighs under her legs and her buttocks, her body cradled in the curve of one of his strong arms. Getting up would be so much harder. She was afraid she would not be able to make that effort to escape him.

He shifted and settled her back into one corner of the chair, still cradled in his arm. He bent and brushed her lips with his, said softly, "Don't be afraid," as if she were a child.

"I am." Her heart was crashing into her ribs. She could feel his hand on her back through the thin cotton of her lacy blouse. One of his fingers, or his thumb, was lying on the bare flesh below her neck and she could feel the touch like a burn.

His lips took hers and she could not stop her head falling back against the softness of the upholstery, her weight going on to his arm. Lips parted, he took her mouth in a deep, shattering kiss. Her hand, trapped between them, found freedom and slipped around his neck, into the waves of his hair.

"I'm not going to hurt you." That was crazy, because he was dangerous, sending her pulses wild and turning her mind to jelly. His lips searched the softness of her cheek, the trembling vulnerability of her closed eyelids, her forehead, and she could feel the yearning, the aching woman's need that had been so long dead inside her.

His mouth traced the line of her throat, the trembling hollow at its base, down to the lacy barrier of the blouse. Such a flimsy thing, the two halves of that light fabric tied together with a long white cord of lace.

His mouth worried at the two loops of the bow lying at the beginning of the cleavage between her breasts. She slid her hand through his hair, her fingers down along the side of his neck, feeling the muscle that jumped there. He lifted his head. He must have caught the end of the cord between his teeth, because she felt it come undone as he raised his head.

He dropped the lace cord against her flesh. His mouth took hers. She could feel the thud of his heart, or hers, as he pulled her against him, her softness pressed flat against his hard chest. Then he released her and she could feel the waiting, needing, knowing.

He was not wearing his jacket, just the shirt. She could feel the heat of him as her palms moved over the smooth fabric. His chest, the bulge of his male breast, his shoulder. Her fingers curled around the curve of his shoulder as his knuckles brushed against her skin just above her bodice. He spread the lacy stuff, pulling the untied cord tight. His fingers traced the small diamonds of flesh exposed on her midriff, seeming to find the sensitive bare flesh unerringly even in the dark.

"So soft," he breathed in a shaken voice. His hand continued down, finding the shape of her hip, her thighs through the skirt spread around her, and he groaned, "I want to feel you, Angela. Your flesh on mine."

She heard the whisper of a groan from her lips, as if his words were his touch. Then, in the dark, he slowly found the two ends of the bow he had untied. He pulled on one and it slid through. She could feel it moving, knew what was happening, and she needed his touch on her bare flesh as she would need water if she were dying in the desert.

He dropped the cord somewhere. Then he spread the blouse and she could feel the cool air on her flesh, but she was hot. Her hands were in his hair when he bent over her and she wasn't sure if she pulled his lips down to the warm curve that was thrust up above her uplift brassière, but she shuddered when their lips touched.

He traced the swelling, found the barrier of her bra. "I knew you would be like this—soft and full. Hot." His teeth found the hard peak of her nipple through the lacy bra and tugged gently.

"Oh! Oh, please..."

Her breathing was sharp, ragged gulps of fire. The front clasp of her bra parted and he closed his free hand around the warm swelling of one full breast. His other hand slid the blouse off one shoulder, caressing the smooth curve of her upper arm as he bared it.

"Kiss me." Was that her voice? A breathless whisper, needing his touch.

He bent over her. His warm fingers shaped her curves. Then his lips covered the swollen peak as the air left her lungs in a rush, a sound like a whimper in her throat. He explored her with his mouth, drawing her inside, and she twisted in his arms.

"I've been aching for you," he murmured, moving his lips from one swollen peak to another. "You're a fever in my blood." His arms shifted to free her from the last entanglement of her bra and he held her, sitting on his lap, his hands sliding along the flesh of her sides as he supported her. His lips moved, seeking in the darkness, found her head dropped back, a pulse beating in her throat.

She had never ached for a man like this before, her body pulsing so heavily, hot with need. She twisted in his grasp and he caressed the long curve of her back, the tender trembling of her midriff, the aching of her aroused breasts.

She closed her hands around his shoulders to keep herself from falling. Then she heard his low demand. "Touch me," he groaned, and she moved to fumble with the buttons of his shirt.

His chest was lightly covered with hair. She slid her palms over it, feeling the tickling of his chest mat against her hands, the hard buttons of his male nipples, aroused.

His palm cupped her hip and he pulled her close, her breasts against his chest, her lips to his. This time the kiss was hard, deep and demanding, leaving her shaken and trembling at the invasion that penetrated to the tight, aching core of her woman's center.

"I need you, Angela."

"Yes." She could not deny what her body had already told him. She felt the hardness of his shoulder muscles. He was wound up tight, aching with what they had stirred in each other.

He lifted her easily, as if she were no weight at all. Oh...

She closed her eyes and buried her face against his neck. He was tense and hard there too. He moved, and there must have been light enough from the moon to guide him.

The stairs.

The fourth step creaked as he stepped on it.

Harvey. Oh, God! Her blouse back there on the carpet somewhere, and her bra. And this man, touching her, claiming her body while Harvey slept only feet away.

"We can't," she whispered.

He took her into her own bedroom. The door was open and he walked in. The whole house seemed half lit with moonlight through the windows. She could see his face, all hard planes and angles, as he bent to lay her on the quilt that covered her bed.

"Not here," she begged. She would never be able to sleep in this bed again without feeling his touch, his lips. She should be able to push him away, but... "Not with Harvey in the house."

He sat beside her. The door was open. She could see the doorway behind him, lightness against shadow. He bent over her and his mouth seduced the curve of her neck. She put her hands up to push him away, but he bent lower, taking the peak of her breast into his mouth, drawing it in, sucking gently and turning her into a mass of trembling need.

When he lifted his head, her fingers were tangled in his hair, clenched tightly.

"Kent..."

He moved to the other breast, but teased lightly this time, his tongue drawing across the hard nub. She could feel it in the pit of her stomach. Then he lifted his head and there was no contact, no touch, only the heavy pulse of passion through her arteries.

Silence, except for her breathing, and his. Then he touched her, his hand shaping her hip intimately, his touch burning through the cotton skirt. His fingers moved to her inner thigh, stilled, curved to the shape of her leg, only an inch from the heated center of her trembling need.

He bent to kiss her lips then, his fingers still. Her body was frozen with waiting, knowing that any second his touch would move to that most vulnerable part of her.

"Just to help you remember," he muttered hoarsely, his mouth leaving hers, then returning. "I don't want you to forget what it is we both need."

Forget? As if he was leaving. She shuddered and he felt how she trembled for his possession. He said, "Tomorrow, when I bring Harvey back from San Francisco."

She swallowed something hard in her throat.

"Be ready. Just a small bag—something for the weekend."

"What?" Was he leaving her like this? How could he, if he felt what she did?

"We're going away." His fingers tightened into the soft flesh of her inner thigh. "You and I, seductive Angela. For the weekend."

He moved and she heard the click of the light switch. The overhead light was glaring, too bright. She blinked and stared up at him.

"I wanted to see you." His eyes were almost black, the blue lost in some emotion. He stared down at her and she could feel her breasts exposed, her lips swollen from his possession.

Harsh light, and she had been in those arms, those lips on her, as if she needed him with desperation beyond anything possible. She wanted to say something, to deny something, everything, but his arm reached out and the darkness returned.

"Tomorrow," his voice promised.

When he was gone, she lay very still. She heard the sound of the door across the hallway opening, then closing. His movements around the room, then silence.

Finally she sat up. There was no sliver of light under the door across the corridor. Her hands went up to cover her breasts in the darkness, and she could feel the aching fullness.

She shuddered and went to her wardrobe, covered herself with the long shield of her dressing gown, still in darkness. Then she stood very still for long moments, but there was no sound from across the hall.

Was he asleep? She was standing, trembling, blood still pulsing through her body, although sanity was returning now. She did not turn on any light, just slipped silently out of her room, along the hallway, down the stairs, missing the one that creaked.

She had to turn on the light to find her things. Her blouse was lying in a pile beside the chair, the bra jumbled with it. She grabbed them and stuffed them inside her robe. If Harvey had seen that——

No one was going to know. How had it happened? So fast. She had been standing there, by the window, and he had come close, just touching. Just light touches, mesmerizing her. She could have pulled back. She could have run, turned on lights and the television, distractions to break that seductive pull.

But she had stood, as if she knew what was coming and wanted it. He had touched, kissed, and she had been in his arms, wanting him to hurry, to bare her flesh and take her body... to love her.

Love. She shuddered. No, it had not been love. He had come for her, for her body. A weekend, he had said, and he would be back. He wanted her, had wanted her from that first contact on the deck of *Misfit*. He did not care who she was, what she was. What *she* wanted.

He was going to have her, possess her. He had stamped his touch on her tonight. To be sure she knew what they both needed, he had said. A weekend.

A few minutes ago, whether Harvey was sleeping down the hall or not, if Kent had not left her room, she would have given him anything, everything he asked.

Hot, passionate, shuddering need. Physical satisfaction, because if he could do this to her, just touching and kissing, then when they made love she would come to the end exhausted, fulfilled. Empty, because it would be the end. Possession. A weekend. What else would be possible between Angela Dalton and a man like Kent Ferguson?

Nothing.

She searched for the cord that had tied her blouse together, but could not find it. She got down on the floor to look under the chair, but it was not there. This was terrible, sneaking around like a teenager trying to hide things from her parents. But she did not want Harvey to know what had happened here, did not want anyone to know...wanted to erase it.

Her glass was on a coffee table near the chair. She could not remember how it had got there. She had been holding it, standing there, then Kent had been close, brushing her flesh with soft, seductive caresses. She had been seduced so easily. Just like the crazy impulsive teenager she had been back when she met Ben Dalton, but Ben's touch had never stirred the kind of explosion that had happened tonight.

She was a grown woman, should have herself under control. She had thought, until tonight, that she did.

Until Kent touched her and something inside had recognized that touch and everything had reached for him, yearned for him.

What had Charlotte said about always picking the wrong men? Angela must have the same problem, because getting involved with Kent Ferguson had to be the most self-destructive thing she could possibly do. He did not belong in her life, and she had no place in his.

She was no young girl dreaming of a knight on a white charger, a Mr. Right. She was old enough to have her dreams sternly attached to reality. She wanted stability, not danger. A man who would be there for her, for their children. She had gambled once on impulse, on passion, and had lost terribly. She would not gamble again. Next time she gave herself, it would be the right man. Maybe the dream was impossible, because she supposed it was a kind, loving knight she wanted. Or nobody.

Kent Ferguson was no knight. He would take what he wanted of her, without giving anything more than physical satisfaction. Then he would be gone. Mr. Wrong.

She drank the glass of flat ginger ale, then took the glass into the kitchen. She did not want to go back upstairs, but if she prowled around here all night he might come down again. Tomorrow, he had said, and a weekend together. She was not going away with him, but she was not fool enough to believe that she could hold out against him in an empty room with only the moon to see, and his touch on her flesh.

She went silently back upstairs. She found a cotton bra and canvas pants, a warm sloppy sweater to go over the pants. She hung the blue skirt and blouse up on the hanger, but without the tie to hold the front together the blouse wanted to slip off the hanger onto the floor.

Just as it had slipped off her, onto the floor, Kent's hands sliding over her skin, hard yet gentle. She shivered and closed the closet door quietly. Let it fall. She would not wear it again.

She remembered her keys as she was on the way downstairs, went back to her room and rummaged in her drawer for the spare keys. The van was at the shop, but the night was quiet and she did not mind the walk at all, needed the air to clear her head.

She went into the kitchen and wrote a short note for Harvey. "Gone to the shop early. Say hello to Charlotte for me." Harvey would wake about seven, and by the time he saw the note he would think she had gone out around dawn, waking early and eager to get to work. It wouldn't be the first time she had done that, although if he knew that she was going to work at three in the morning, he would wonder what was going on.

In the empty shop, she brewed a pot of coffee. With the lights on, the doors locked and the world dark outside, she was alone in the universe. She moved about, setting her mug down here and there as she picked up scraps of Sunbrella and canvas, bits of thread. By five in the morning, darkness outside still, she had the place looking as tidy as if she were going away for a week.

She poured another cup of the coffee, faintly bitter now, and went upstairs to where she had her pattern paper and a dressmaker's model. Last month, a woman who owned one of Angela's fishermen's shirts had gone to great lengths to find a pair of pants to match in Seattle. Since then two of the woman's friends had been into the shop, asking if she could make them something similar. There was obviously a market, and Angela suspected several of the boating women would quite willingly shell out for a complete matching outfit: Sailing Rags pants and shirt and matching carry-all bag.

The problem was, it was much easier to design a shirt that would fit everyone in one of three sizes than it was pants. A design that would look good and feel comfortable.

When she looked up from her paper and pins and scissors, there was light streaming in through the window. Another sunny day, probably with yesterday's blustery wind.

A good day for flying.

She was not going to think about him. All that mattered was Harvey's meeting with Charlotte, and she hoped that went well. Kent was Charlotte's—just a relative of Charlotte's. That was *all* he was! Damn it, she was *not* going to spend the day remembering last night, Kent's voice low and seductive, his touch, his lips...

She jabbed a pin viciously into the paper. She had already gone in circles with her mind, walking to the shop in the dark, trying desperately to think of an airtight way of dealing with Kent when he returned. Thinking in circles "Be ready." "Just a small bag." "We're going away... for the weekend."

She was *not* going away with him. He certainly could not force her, but he would make it very awkward, walking in here and saying let's go, as if he had a right and that of course she was coming. Knowing that he was bloody near irresistible.

Damn it, he hadn't even asked her! Just assumed, said pack a bag, and then he'd walked out, leaving her lying there like a fool. Wanting him.

She was realizing just how clever he was at manipulating people, and she knew she did not want to face him down. She wanted a foolproof way to avoid the whole issue.

She had no idea how long it took to fly to San Francisco, but it had to be at least a couple of hours, perhaps more. Even if they left at dawn, there was no way they'd be back until midafternoon, probably much later. She would work on the design for the canvas pants, and some time between now and midafternoon the answer would come to her.

She hoped.

Barney came in at eight. She heard the door downstairs, and tensed because it could be Harvey, and Kent might be with him. Then she heard the tuneless whistle and called out, "Up here, Barney! I'm in the loft."

He came up the stairs, noisy in his boots. "At it early, aren't you? In a creative rage?"

Angela leaned back on her heels and stared at the paper pattern hanging on the model. "What do you think?"

He laughed. "One good rainstorm and they'll fall apart. Can't make pants out of paper."

She stuck her tongue out at him. "How are Sally and the baby? Where's Jake?"

"I left Jake with the sitter today. Sally's coming home Monday."

Too bad it wasn't today. Angela could have used it as an excuse to leave the shop, to help Sally settle in at home with the new baby. She muttered, "Dad's gone to San Francisco with Kent Ferguson," managing to say his name as if he were a stranger. Maybe she wasn't quite so badly rattled by him as she had thought. She tried to ignore a flash of memory, herself lying half naked on her own bed, staring up at him, seeing him looking at her, his eyes claiming what he saw.

She had thought she knew what physical desire was, but intimacy with Ben had been tame compared to what had happened in her blood under Kent Ferguson's eyes.

Barney's smile was fading. He pushed his hands through his hair, said, "The bombshell? Jeez, Angie, don't you think Dad's better off without her?"

"I don't know." She sighed. "It's Harvey's decision, isn't it? Are you sure you're not just worried because you don't want anyone in your mother's place?"

"Ouch!" muttered Barney. "Casting me as the selfish son?" He kicked at a scrap on the floor.

She shrugged and half smiled. "If the shirt fits."

"Yeah." He prowled through her cuttings of paper. "Maybe there is some of that, but I just figure that about the time Dad thinks he has hold of her forever, she'll disappear again." Defensively, he added, "She's nothing like Mom."

"Maybe he has to have someone different. A woman like Anna would always be competing with her in our minds, in his mind."

He wandered off into the shop, thinking about it. A moment later he shouted up, "I'm throwing this coffee out! It's terrible. I'll make another pot."

The customers started coming and Angela had to leave her pattern. Through the morning, in between customers, she worked on making half a dozen sheet bags out of the scraps from the last dodger job. The bags were tough and lined with plastic inside, made to snap on cabin sides and hold the coil of rope from the sails. She could have sold more of them, they were always in demand, but she used scraps to keep the price down, limiting her production by the amount of scrap cuttings available.

A scraggy, bearded man burst into the shop just before noon. "I've got a torn mains'l. Can you fix it?" He stood, looking at the assortment of products around him, not looking at her, but waiting for an answer. "From leech to luff," he grumbled. "Got caught in a gale out by Cape Flattery—running. She gybed on me, tore it all to hell."

Angela left the machine and reached for the ringing telephone as she told him, "You'd better take it to the sail-makers. There's a loft down at Point Hudson."

Charlotte's voice on the telephone, breathless and panicked. "Angie?"

"I'll have one of these," said the scraggly beard. He dropped a blue sheet bag onto the counter.

"Just a minute," she told Charlotte, then gave the sailor the price. He dug through a battered, salt-stained wallet, digging out wilted notes while Charlotte's voice hurried on in her ear.

"He's here, Angie. He—— Oh, I don't know what to do! The two of them together. Kent phoned up from the lobby. Kent! And Harvey's with him."

"Thanks," Angela told the sailor.

"What am I going to do?" wailed Charlotte.

Angela bit her lip. "Couldn't you see them?"

"Together?"

"Charlotte, look ... Well, why don't you just come clean with them both? Get it over with." Lord knew where she got off, giving advice. It seemed to Angela that Charlotte was creating her own problems, but after last night she was in no position to criticize.

"How can I? I—there's just no way. For one thing, Mom would kill me. I thought—I thought when I took off—I didn't think Harvey would come after me!"

Charlotte was fifty-one. Angela would have thought it was high time she stopped feeling afraid of her mother. It wasn't all that surprising, really, that Kent had sounded exasperated when he came to take the boat home. Picking up Charlotte's messes could get tiresome after a few times.

Charlotte said, "If Harvey would just forget me..."

Angela sighed. "You don't know Harvey very well if you expect that." Her father-in-law might be a quiet, gentle man, but he could be stubbornly persistent when it suited him. "If you want to get rid of him, you'll have to tell him so yourself." There was a pause on the telephone, silence with sounds filtering through from the background. "Charlotte, where are you? In your hotel room?"

"I'm across the street, in a phone booth. When Kent called up to my room, I—I went out the back way. But I left my purse up there, and my passport. If I didn't have my calling card number memorized, I wouldn't even be able to call you."

"You could have called me collect." It had been stupid of them to turn up together, making Charlotte feel hemmed in and threatened. Of course, neither of them would know that. They had come, and Charlotte had run again, with Kent and Harvey in pursuit.

Easy enough to call Charlotte a coward, but Angela herself was plotting ways to disappear when Kent came back to Port Townsend later today. And if Charlotte was running from Mr. Right, while she was running from Mr. Wrong and the traditional fate worse than death, it didn't really make any difference, did it? They were both cowards.

CHAPTER FIVE

RUNNING. That was the thing that got Angela in the end. She didn't have to run from anyone! Didn't she pride herself on being strong and decisive and...?

Vulnerable. Shivering in his arms...waiting...wanting.

No, damn it! She wasn't going to be ruled by hormones and a man with too damned much sex appeal! And she definitely was not going to run away.

She sewed the windshield on to the top section of a dodger, took it all down to the sailboat it belonged on and found that she had everything about an inch too big. Better too big than too small, but she should have checked it first, made one more trip down to the boat to clamp everything in place and be sure before she put on trim and sewed seams.

She had the long seam ripped out, the fabric cut back, and the new trim sewn on when he came through the door. Kent. Just Kent, alone.

She bent her head to the machine. The black binding was over her right shoulder, the windshield under her left arm. She pulled on the trim and the spool over her head uncoiled another turn or two. She folded the trim over the edge of the windshield, pushed her foot down on the drive and sewed six inches of trim before she said a word to him.

He had stopped at the counter, one hand in his pocket. He was, as always, perfectly dressed, the suit emphasizing the broad shoulders subtly.

"Where's Dad?" was what she finally said.

"San Francisco."

"Was Charlotte there?"

He shrugged. "She's still registered at the hotel."

So Harvey was waiting, hoping Charlotte would come back to her hotel room. And Charlotte would have to eventually, because she had left her wallet and her passport behind.

Angela pushed the drive pedal again and powered over another foot of binding. Her heart was smashing into her rib cage and she could feel the trembling even down in her foot, making the machine surge and ebb. She stared at the walking foot of the machine, watched as it advanced and pulled the fabric step by step. When she lifted her foot, everything was silent.

If she sat here, afraid of him, afraid of the effect of a touch, a look, he was going to know. He probably knew anyway.

When she turned around, he was examining one of the sheet bags, not looking at her at all. Then he looked across at her, the bag in his hands. "What's this for?"

She pulled on the binding streaming over her shoulder, unwinding it from the spool above, giving herself more room to move. Rope to hang herself, she thought wildly. "It's for rope, sail sheets. A place to get them out of the way." She swallowed. "That one—— Those long, skinny pockets in the back, I made them to store winch handles."

He turned the bag in his hands, tested the pocket with his hand, checking its strength or the workmanship. "You do neat work."

"Thanks." Neat! The windshield was a mess, and upstairs the paper pattern for canvas pants was just a hopeless jumble.

"What time are you finished in here?"

She swallowed. Did he think she had a suitcase packed, ready for a weekend with him? "I—I'm not going anywhere with you." Her voice sounded sharp, high and panicked. "If you've come here for me, you're—I'm not going away with you."

She curled her fingers around the binding that was streaming over her shoulders, across her front to the machine. Why didn't he say something? She blurted nervously, "I don't want an affair with you."

There was nothing at all to be read in his face. Empty, but harsh, his mouth a hard line. She smoothed the binding she had crumpled in her fingers.

"Fair enough." He dropped the sheet bag onto the shelf where he had found it. She thought he might have sounded more upset if a waitress told him he couldn't have the lobster he had ordered. He shrugged. "Harvey said to tell you he'd call tonight."

She heard a crash from the shop. The door opened and Barney came in, his welding mask tipped up, his shirt and pants and face black from the steel he had been working on.

Barney's voice had that strained quality that revealed his feelings. "Ferguson—you're back. Where's Dad?"

"San Francisco." Kent took one look around the room—Barney, the sheet bags, a display of T-shirts, a rack of Sunbrella and canvas in a variety of colors. Angela and her machines with the mess around them.

"Goodbye," he said then. "I'll be off."

Was that all? Was he simply going to leave?

He turned and walked out, and she stared through the window at the red Chevette until it reversed out of their little parking lot. Gone. He really hadn't wanted her that badly. He had not put up an argument at all, had not come close to brush those long fingers over her cheek. After last night, he had to know that he could make her tremble for him with just the lightest touch, but he had not even tried.

Barney laughed and she turned to stare at him.

"Talkative devil, isn't he? If Fergusons have to marry into our family, I'd far rather it was Charlotte! Look, Angie, I'm going to clean up and get out of here. I've got to see Sally and the baby at the hospital."

"Go ahead."

Marry. Charlotte had run at the thought, and the last thing Kent wanted was to marry. If he ever married, she'd be willing to bet it would be all thought out ahead, debits and credits, and the woman would be a good bargain, an asset. Ben had been so impulsive it was ridiculous, jerking all around the country in a crazy life where everything but the trailer was transient. Not Kent. Impulsive was the last thing he could be called.

He was gone. That was all that mattered.

Harvey called that night after she got to the house.

"Angie? She finally came back to the hotel. I—we're having dinner. I might—well, I might not be back for a while. I think I'll stay here and——"

"It's okay, Dad." If Harvey wanted to have an affair out of sight of his family, to have some time alone with Charlotte, he certainly didn't have to explain to his daughter-in-law. "Give Charlotte my love. And have a good time."

That was the last she heard from him for six days. She finished the dodger and worked out the canvas pants. She washed a section of eight-ounce canvas to shrink it, then threw it in the dryer with fabric softener, then started cutting. She made the first pair for herself, wore them for a day and decided to change the design of the pockets.

Sally got the second pair. She loved them. Angela made the third pair for a customer who came in asking about canvas clothes. Then she laid out for a complete set, one in each of four sizes, to send down to the shop in Seattle that handled her fishermen's shirts.

It was a quiet week, customers everywhere, but none of it seeming to penetrate her thoughts. She kept expecting Kent to walk back in. He didn't. Just a man wanting a dodger repaired right away, because he wanted to go sailing on Saturday. Another sailor with a broken motor mount that Barney looked after. An order for sail covers for a big ketch.

Harvey on the telephone.

"Angie? Look—er—we're going down to Cabo San Lucas for a couple of weeks. Could you dig my passport out and express it to me here at the Sheraton?" He sounded slightly embarrassed, but happy. "And—er—could you tell Barney? A week. Maybe two weeks."

"Enjoy yourself," said Angela softly. She hoped it would work out. She didn't want Harvey hurt. If Charlotte gave him a fling, an affair, and then walked out on him...

"Yeah." Harvey coughed.

"And give Charlotte my love."

Two weeks. It seemed insane to keep expecting Kent to come through that door, but she did.

He came, finally, on a rainy Friday afternoon in the last week of August. Barney was down on the waterfront with the portable welder. Harvey was presumably still in Mexico with Charlotte. Sally was home with Jake and the new baby.

Angela was the only one in the shop. She was cutting out the pattern pieces for pants in eight-ounce canvas. She had only been interrupted twice all afternoon. Even the customers weren't interested in browsing or looking for repairs with the rain pounding down in a twenty-knot wind.

When the door opened, a twist of wind blew in the rain. She looked up and saw the back of a man's head, the back of a light brown raincoat as he pulled against the wind to force the door closed.

Kent. She shifted the pattern piece and pulled two pins out of her pincushion. It was not a good sign when she recognized the man from the back of his head.

"Did you come looking for Charlotte?" She was relieved to find her voice steady and calm.

He took off his raincoat and laid it on the counter.

"You could hang that up on the hook behind the desk." Now why the hell had she said that? It was almost an invitation for him to come in and stay a while.

He left the coat where it was, and came around the end of the display shelves. He was wearing a brown sweater with an open-necked shirt underneath. Except for that night in her living room, it was the first time she had seen him without a tie.

"Charlotte's not here."

"I know." He walked along the cutting table, watching as she pinned the pattern down and started cutting. "Do you ever relax? Every time I come in here, you're hard at it."

"What about you?" She didn't realise the smile was coming until she felt her lips curl. "Do you take a lot of holidays? I bet you don't. You're in the office Sundays, and five o'clock some mornings."

He leaned one hip against the cutting table. "What makes you think that?"

"I don't know." She studied him—the eyes, the mouth. "There's nothing frivolous about you. You have the look of a man who eats for body fuel only and doesn't get enough fun in his life."

"Close." He picked up a scrap of the canvas and rubbed his thumb over the rough texture. "You could change that."

"I doubt it." That kind of thought would be dangerous. She knew better than to try to change a man. She snipped around a curve.

He shrugged. "I'm wet and hungry. Come out to dinner with me."

She glanced through the window behind him, the white car sitting in the rain. "That's not a rental car?" It was the kind of car he would own, white and expensive. "I'm sure it's got a good heater, and you only got wet coming from the car to here. You drove, didn't you? Did you come across on the ferry from Keystone?"

"Yes. I'm starved." He ran his fingers along the fabric on the table. She remembered those fingers, touching her.

"There's a McDonald's across the street. You can take me there for dinner if you want." She smiled, knowing he would turn that down. It was hardly his style!

"I thought somewhere with candlelight." He moved away from the table. "Music, dancing."

"Sorry." Dancing, his arms around her. "I'm just closing. I'm going to McDonald's. You can go where you want."

"Big Macs and fries for supper, then. Let's go."

Startled, she stared at him. "You're serious? I—I was trying to put you off."

"I know. Do you have a raincoat?"

"Yes." Her heart was doing it again, thundering in her ears while her mind painted pictures, sensations. She whispered, "In the back."

"Get it, then."

When she came back, Kent was waiting at the door for her. He held the door, then took her keys out of her hand to lock up for her. "Did you think I was too much of a snob for a fast-food joint?"

"Yes," she admitted, flushing.

He gave a snort of laughter. "Are you always so blunt? No, stay here under cover while I get the car open."

"You're not driving? It's only across the street! We can walk."

"We'd be soaked."

She huddled under the awning, hugging her raincoat to herself, watching through the rain as he ran to his white car and quickly unlocked it. He did not open the passenger door for her at once, but reversed and pulled up right beside her.

"Come on! Hop in!"

This was crazy. Why had she said yes? Or had she? She slid into the car, pulled the door closed and stared through the windshield, feeling the intimacy of being shut inside such a small space with him. The last thing she needed was to share a meal with him.

He gave his attention to driving in the poor visibility. Even when he stopped at the intersection to the highway, he did not look at her, but at the highway traffic, waiting for a break to cross to the fast-food outlet.

Angela was silent. What on earth were they going to talk about? They had nothing in common besides Charlotte and Harvey... except for the explosion that had happened two weeks ago in the darkness.

Why was he here?

He took her arm and hurried her inside out of the rain. "What do you want? I'll order while you find us a table."

She thought of insisting that she pay her own share, knew he would object and decided that it would not be worth the hassle. She found an empty table near the window, between three teenage boys talking in low voices, and an elderly woman reading a paperback book.

Kent unloaded the tray on their table, looked down at the plastic packages that held his hamburger and her chicken nuggets. "You're sure you wouldn't rather have a nice steak somewhere? Or a lasagna...maybe lobster?"

She smiled up at him. He really did look out of place. "What do you propose to do? Throw this all out?"

He had a surprisingly nice smile, wide and rather shattering. "Give it to those teenagers," he suggested. She shook her head, laughing, and he sat down across from her. His leg brushed her knee under the table as he sat down.

She opened her package of mustard sauce and dipped a chicken piece into it. "It's not the menu I was after when I suggested this place." She concentrated on the piece of chicken. He picked up his hamburger.

"You're dripping," she said, handing him a napkin.

"Hmm." He caught the drip and took a bite of the hamburger. "I bet it was the bright lights you wanted. Don't you trust me in the dark?"

She could feel the heat rising in her face, but she answered, "Not as far as I could throw you. I'd be crazy, wouldn't I? And don't look so pleased with yourself. You may be very..." she gulped "...persuasive, but I'm not—er——"

He nodded, said soberly, "I believe you don't want to be interested."

She looked past him, found one of the teenage boys watching her. "Don't you have a girlfriend in Vancouver?"

"Nobody that matters."

She swallowed, knowing that was exactly the point. Nobody that mattered. She would not matter either, not afterward. She could see the future, a forecast of her own doom. She could not bear it to happen again, to stand alone and watch a man she cared about walk away with her heart.

Damn! She jabbed another chicken piece into the mustard sauce. "Have you heard from Charlotte?" she asked.

"Not directly." He was demolishing his hamburger. "But she's been using her credit cards. Mexico."

"Hmm. Cabo San Lucas—she and Harvey went down there together."

"Ah, so he did catch up with her in San Francisco. That's good."

She blinked. "Do you actually approve of Charlotte and Harvey?"

"Why not?"

"Well, I—I just thought—Harvey's not exactly...I didn't think you'd really approve."

He frowned as he wiped his mouth with the napkin. "You had visions of my paying Harvey off to get rid of him, get him out of my sister's life?"

She nodded, knowing she had misjudged him.

He asked reasonably, "Why did you think I took him to find her?"

"I don't know. I thought—well, I just thought there must be some reason." She realized that her fingers were tearing up one of the chicken pieces and stopped abruptly, dropping the chicken back into its plastic tray.

"Some devious reason?"

"I suppose so." She had thought Charlotte was only an excuse, that Kent had come to seduce her.

His brows were thick over his eyes, darker than his hair, shadowing whatever she might have seen in the blue of his gaze. His hand moved, reaching for hers.

She jerked her hand off the table. He had watched her from the beginning. He had waited in the dark for her to return from Charles. Waited for her. She had not really been surprised to find him there. It was almost inevitable, given that powerful awareness between them.

She pushed her hands through her hair, sending the curls wild. "Can we talk about something else? Anything else?"

He did not answer. She knew he could see her discomfort. He was watching her, always watching. His hand was lying on the table between them, those long, strong fingers. If she put her hand back up, he would take it with his. As long as she avoided his touch, she seemed to keep some degree of sanity. Not much, but enough, she hoped.

"Did you read that?" he asked.

She blinked in confusion. "What? Read what?"

"That book?" He gestured toward the woman across from them.

"Oh." A neutral topic. She swallowed again, wishing she could get rid of the lump in her throat. "Yes, I did." She tidied her hair roughly with her hands. She was restless, could hardly sit still. Kent seemed just the opposite, as if he could sit there forever.

"What did you think of it?"

"I——" She had to get hold of herself. "I didn't like it much. I read his first two and loved them. When that came out, I bought it right away. Even paid for the hardcover because I didn't want to wait for it to come out in paperback."

"Yeah, me too." He was rubbing his thumb and forefinger together, an absent motion. "Twenty-seven dollars, and I couldn't even finish it. I got to page two hundred and finally gave up, still waiting for the action to start. As a thriller, it was a dead loss."

"I finished it." She peeled the paper off her straw and started sipping her Coke.

"Did the story ever get off the ground?"

She took a deep breath, felt the tension flowing away. She grinned. "Introspective agonizing right through to the end. Edmund was still waffling around like Hamlet on the last page."

His laughter made the woman with the book look up sharply. "Next time I'll wait for the paperback."

"Or borrow it," she suggested.

"Better," he agreed.

He mentioned another author, then somehow they were in a discussion of the merits of a recent film version of an Alistair MacLean adventure and she said, "I don't see you lining up for the cinema."

"Popcorn and noisy teenagers in the front rows? No, you're right. I rent videos. I have a weakness for watching television in bed at night—helps me sleep."

"Alone?" Why had she asked that? She panicked, trying to look away from his eyes, finding her gaze locked on his long fingers as they crumpled his used napkin, seeing the blond hairs growing on the back of his hand.

"Usually," he said quietly.

"Not like Charlotte," she said brightly. She pushed her hand through her hair, shook it slightly. "Charlotte hates doing anything alone." She realized then that they had been talking about sleeping alone, and said abruptly, "Movies, I mean. Or...anything. You—you and Charlotte aren't much alike, though, are you?"

"Not much." She could see the amusement in his eyes. So he knew how flustered she was. What a stupid question, whether he watched those movies alone...in bed.

"Except for your eyes," she muttered. She blinked her own. "You've both got blue eyes. And her hair must have been blonde, before it went gray." What had they been talking about before she made such a stupid comment? Cinema? Movies. She tried to think of one single thing to say and came up with a total blank.

He caught the hand in her hair and pulled it away. "Stop it, Angela."

"What?" A whisper. She pressed her lips together and swallowed.

His fingers tightened on her hand. "Why are you afraid of me?"

She shook her head mutely.

He sighed. "All right—Charlotte. We'll talk about my sister if you want. And no, it's not a family resemblance. I'm adopted."

"But——" It was Charlotte's secret, not hers to tell. She looked away in confusion, her hand still caught in his.

"A friend of my mother's," he said dryly. "A school friend."

"What?" She shook her head in confusion. "I lost you somewhere."

His lips quirked. "Angela, I'm trying to find a topic of conversation that will let you relax."

She pulled and he let her hand free. She met his eyes. "I know I'm acting like a fool. I—you——"

"Yeah." For a second she thought he would reach for her hand again, but he didn't. The blue of his eyes was almost black. "Me, too. Why else do you think I'm resorting to my own doubtful beginnings as a topic of conversation?"

"Doubtful?" She frowned, knowing this was the last thing she should be talking about with him.

"My natural mother was a school friend of my mother's—my adoptive mother's, that is. That's really all I know."

Unwillingly, fascinated, she protested, "But surely—haven't you ever asked your...your mother—who your real mother is, I mean?"

"It's not the sort of thing you talk about to my mother. It makes her uneasy, and she doesn't answer in any case. For all I know, it could be someone I've known all my life, one of Mother's bridge friends." He frowned. "Or a total stranger. It doesn't matter."

She thought he had told himself that many times, wondered if he really believed he didn't care. "Your father——"

"The only thing my father ever talked about was real estate. And money. It's amazing, really, that a free spirit like Charlotte came out of those two."

"You——" She shook her head, really confused now. "I thought you didn't think much of Charlotte."

"I think she's exasperating." He scowled, then admitted, "When I was a kid, I used to think she was magic. I didn't see her much. She's sixteen years older, never lived in our house as long as I can remember. She turned up occasionally, turned the dull sobriety of our house upside-down for a few days, then disappeared again."

"House." She closed her eyes, knowing the other side of this from Charlotte's confessions. "You said *house*. As if—— Why don't you say home?"

He frowned. She knew the answer, but he was not going to say it. She whispered, "Charlotte felt that way too. She always wanted a home. Somehow, it seemed impossible to her." She touched his hand tentatively. "Your parents were very cold people, weren't they?" Cruel too, she thought, although perhaps they had not meant to be.

He did not return her grasp, but said rather grimly, "If so, that makes me more their natural child than Charlotte, doesn't it?"

"No." He wasn't cold. He might wear a mask, and she could understand why. Every child wanted approval, and with parents like his, there would be only one way to win their smiles. But inside the cool mask...

She pulled her hand back from his. "Do you like theater? Live, I mean? Performances out under the stars?"

The darkness faded from his eyes and he was the cool man, totally in control, but she could see through the mask now. "I haven't been to a live play in years. I used to like it, back in college."

"There's a theater festival on here this week."

"Why don't we go?" His eyes locked on hers.

The woman with the book was gone, and the teenagers. Outside, it was dark. They had been sitting here for over an hour, talking across plastic cartons and empty soft drinks.

He caught her hand, turned it palm up and traced a line softly through the center of her palm. "I think we'd both enjoy the theater together, Angela."

She should pull her hand away, but somehow her brain would not send the right instruction to her muscles.

"I don't think——" Yet she had been the one to bring up the subject of the theater, as if it were an invitation.

"Why not?" He was watching with that grim intensity again, as if he could read the thoughts right out of her mind.

He let go of her hand, or she pulled away—she was not sure which. She picked up his empty paper cup and stacked it with hers. "There's no point in it. We—— Why don't you just go back to Vancouver and...ask someone there? There's got to be any number of women who——"

"Any number," he agreed. "Dozens—hundreds, maybe. Agreeable, good-looking, intelligent." She saw a muscle jerk in his jaw. "They don't happen to be the ones keeping me awake nights."

She could feel the heat rising in her, the memory of her own sleepless nights. She whispered, "Have you tried them?"

He smiled wryly. "There's no point, is there? It would be like eating chocolate when what you crave is ice cream."

Which was she? Chocolate? Or ice cream? What if she went to the theater with him? She caught her hand trembling and pushed it back into her lap. The theater. It sounded harmless, and with any other man it would be. But even a theater date with Kent and she would be lost. He was way out of her league. Not a Charles to be enjoyed without risk.

She had spent the last two weeks waiting for him to come back, thinking, deciding and deciding again. He would ask and she would say no. Or she would say yes. She was an adult woman, and if she decided to have a discreet affair with Kent Ferguson...if he came asking again...who would be harmed?

In one of those fits of temptation, she had gone to her doctor, but afterward she had known it was impossible. She knew who would be hurt. Not Kent. Just Angela, when it was over. Angela's affair, but she had never done anything like that before. She would go up in flames, and afterward there would be only ashes. He had told her he dreamed of her, but she was pretty sure that when he possessed what he wanted, his dreams would stop.

Hers wouldn't.

Why was he watching her? Had he said something? If so, she had not heard the words. She piled the cups on top of the plastic dishes. "I don't want you in my life." She sucked in her breath and avoided his eyes. "I don't want an affair with you." She felt foolish, because he had said the theater, and it was she who was talking about making love.

She was safe on her side of the table, she thought wildly, just out of arm's reach. They were in bright light, with two noisy couples sitting just behind Kent. It had to be one of the least romantic places in the world. As long as he couldn't touch her, surely he couldn't weave her in his web?

He leaned forward. His voice was low, carrying only to her. "Angela, you're lying. You want it, maybe as much as I do."

She stared down at her hands, began mechanically moving the litter in front of her. His hands came over hers, stilling them. A lie. Yes. She was afraid of what would happen if she became involved with him, but she could not forget the touch of his hands, the caress of his lips, the shattering feel of his body holding hers hard. And it was a good thing that there was this table between them, because she knew she could not trust herself with him.

That was why she had gone to the doctor last week, for insurance. If she . . . if they—well, whatever happened, the only consequences would be inside her head when he left.

She muttered, "Don't touch me."

He was angry, his eyes hardening, his voice dangerously soft. "What do you think I am? Think back, Angela. That was you in my arms in your living room. You begging me to kiss your breasts, you pulling——"

She jerked and her hands were free, flung out, a barrier that was no barrier at all. Abruptly, he stood. She got up too, picking up the mess at their table, stacking it onto the tray. He took the tray from her and she followed him to the litter bin where he shoved the whole thing in with a jerk.

Outside, where it was still raining, she started out into the downpour.

"Stay there!" he snapped. "I'll bring the car."

"No! I—I'll walk back."

"Don't be an idiot!" He stormed off toward the car, his raincoat flapping around his legs. He hadn't done his coat up, and the rain was fiercer than ever, bouncing off the pavement.

When she got in his car, she could feel his anger. She had not expected anger from him, had not really thought it would matter to him that much. He started the car with a jerk.

She said harshly, "Just let me off at the shop."

"I'll drive you home."

She would be at home without a car if he did. She stared through the windshield and said nothing, wondered if he could see as little as she could. She remembered then that Harvey was away, that she was alone in the house. That knowledge seemed to knock the ability to think right out of her.

When he stopped the car at her house, it was still going around in circles. Harvey gone. The house empty. Kent, wanting her. He pushed the car in to park and got out, and she just sat there in his car under the roof of the old carriage house that was a garage now.

Kent. How could a woman get in this state about a man she hardly knew? But he did not feel like a stranger, hadn't from that first shocking impact of his blue eyes on her. What if he went inside with her? She knew what would happen, but what about the morning? Would she be free of this insane yearning? Or trapped forever?

He opened her door, and she got out, stumbling when he took her arm to hurry her to the veranda.

"Your key?" The porch light seemed to make a halo around him, some weird effect of light through water drops, because this man was no angel.

She stared at his chin and kept her voice steady. "Kent, I don't want you to come inside."

He put his hands in the pockets of his raincoat. He looked bigger than usual in the bulky sweater and raincoat. She wondered what it would feel like to be crushed against his chest with the rain lying on his clothes.

"You know, Angela, your behavior doesn't make a lot of sense."

She shuddered. "You should look at it from this side."

He jerked his head to throw back a damp lock of hair from his forehead. "I suspect it's too late for me to get off this peninsula on the ferry."

"As a bid to get inside, that's pretty obvious. I'm supposed to take pity on you, invite you into my parlor."

"It would be nice." He touched her cheek softly. "You're not going to leave me out here, are you?"

Arrogant, she thought. Taking her for granted. "I didn't issue any invitations. The last ferry to Keystone doesn't go until quarter to nine."

"It's nine now."

How could it be? They had just gone to dinner. Surely they hadn't talked for three hours?

He held his hand out for the key again. "Can I come in?"

If she wanted to commit an indiscretion, this had to be the perfect opportunity—Harvey gone, the house empty. No one to care.

It seemed cold-blooded, his coming down here to try to get her into bed. More cold-blooded, standing out here skirting around it while he tried to talk his way inside. He was manipulating her, but if he touched her, even the slightest brush of his flesh on hers, she knew she would be lost.

She wrapped her arms around herself and admitted, "You're right, I'm not consistent. And...and yes, I'm tempted, but I'm not asking you in. I got myself into one hellish mess years ago by...by letting myself get carried away." She sucked in a deep breath. "I'm *never* going to let that happen to me again!"

He was suddenly very quiet, those eyes watching her as if she were a rival for a piece of property he wanted. Assessing. Looking for weaknesses? She shivered.

"Your husband," he said at last, pulling the answer out of the air, she thought wildly. "It wasn't all roses and love and happy ever after?"

She did not want to talk about this, giving him pieces of herself, making it harder to keep him out. He pushed his hands into his pockets and she managed to breathe again.

His voice was very reasonable. "Haven't you got this out of proportion, Angela?" She decided this must be the voice he used to negotiate a land deal. "We're not talking about permanence here. We're talking you and me, and what's unfinished between us."

She met his eyes. "Making love?"

"Put whatever name you want on it." He shrugged. "I want to go to bed with you. You want it too. If you're afraid there's more to it, you can quit worrying."

She laughed painfully. "You're a cold bastard."

"So I've been told." He sounded bored and she knew it was really anger, and the danger was over now. "Give me your key."

She rummaged for it, moved toward the door, only to have him grab the key away from her. He fitted it in the door, but could not make the lock turn. He muttered something under his breath.

"You've got to lift up on the door. It's a bit temperamental."

He lifted. "Temperamental? Not unlike the mistress of the house, is it?"

She took the key from him, a little afraid to step past him. Was he going to come in after all?

"Get in!" he snapped.

She did not move. She wanted to say something, but had no idea what words.

"Did you want to change your mind?" Kent demanded. "If you don't want me in your bed, you'd better get through that door. Otherwise I'm going to assume that you're inviting me in and I'll——"

She moved. She started to turn back as she got inside, found herself facing the door itself as he slammed it shut behind her. A lucky escape—she told herself that. Lucky to have got away, because he could have turned her will-power to jelly easily enough. It was almost as if he had not really tried.

Outside, Kent stared at the door he had slammed. The whole day was crazy, from the lunch meeting that he had abruptly left to drive down here to the way he had deliberately angered Angela just now, here on her own veranda.

He never had troubles with women, usually knew instinctively how to handle a situation. Not that he was a womanizer, there wasn't time for that with all the odds and ends of the empire his father had left. But, God! He usually had a bit more finesse than this! Bluntly telling her he wanted her in bed, challenging her when she as much as admitted she was nervous of the explosive thing between them.

Nervous! Hell, if she felt the way he did, she must be terrified. He had never felt so undone over a woman, from that first meeting. Time hadn't made any difference. Or other women. He had realized over these last two weeks that nothing was going to get rid of this itch except scratching it. Make love to Angela, satisfy the urge, instead of ignoring it.

So he had come down here and come on to Angela like a stupid adolescent, about as subtle as a steamroller. It wouldn't have taken a lot of finesse, for heaven's sake! She was attracted too. She needed bright lights to ward off the danger. Look at what had happened two weeks ago! He'd just touched her, meaning to kiss her and lead into something more—a date. The beginning of a seduction, yes, but taking his time, not jumping all over her like a horny rabbit.

But that first kiss had exploded, and it hadn't been just him. She had been incredible, that husky, vulnerable gasp deep in her throat, the wonderful warm softness of her. He'd lost it completely, had hardly known where he was until he had her lying on her own bed, himself bending over her with nothing but the glory of sharing that wonderful loving with her.

It had been some sound that had jerked him to his senses. A bedspring somewhere, Harvey down the hallway. The awareness that they were not alone, that if he bent to her naked softness he would be lost. Maybe lost forever.

Leaving her there, alone in her bed, had been the hardest thing he had ever done in his life. He had thought of little else all the way to San Francisco on the Lear, and back north. Angela. He would take her somewhere they could be alone, away from everyone they knew. He would touch her, kiss her, and she would turn to a flaming temptress in his arms.

He had wanted her with an intensity that terrified him. The fear was strong enough that when he came back to Dalton Welding and Canvas that afternoon, back to take her away, he had felt relief when she said she was not going anywhere with him. Despite the fever in him, he knew that everything about her was too much, from her outspoken way of opposing him at every turn to his own violent reactions. He did not like the wheeling-out-of-control sensation.

It was sex—hormones. Something about her that put it all together with a force no other woman had for him.

He went back to his car, telling himself he'd had a lucky escape. The last thing he needed was his life turned upside-down, cool reality turned to blazing need. After this fiasco, it was past time he found other ways to get Angela out of his dreams.

CHAPTER SIX

"YOUR sister on line three." Patricia's voice was non-committal.

Kent picked up the receiver, disturbed because she never called him this way, always used telegrams or post-cards. Hell, in San Francisco he'd suspected that Charlotte had dodged out of her hotel room more to avoid him than Harvey.

She sounded nervous. Listening to her uneasy breathing over the telephone line, he realized suddenly that he was tired of the tension in his family. Mother and Charlotte, the angry tension between them—he had always kept aloof from them both. Impossible to be close to his mother, of course, but Charlotte...

"Charlotte, are you all right?"

"Yes. Oh, yes, I am." She sounded nervous, though. Hell, she always seemed nervous around him. Come to that, so did Angela. What kind of image did he project, anyway, to drive personal relationships away so effectively?

"Where are you, Charlotte?"

"Port Townsend. I...I'm married."

"Harvey?" How the hell was he ever going to get Angela out of his dreams now? "Congratulations, Charlotte. He's a good man."

"Yes, but—Mother's not going to be very happy."

Probably not. Her daughter married to a welder. Kent sighed. "I'll talk to her, shall I?" A retired businessman, that would go over better with Mother.

"I—yes. Please...and...Kent, could you come down here? To Port Townsend. This weekend...please?"

Port Townsend. Angela. Every time he saw her, she haunted him with fresh power. He could feel his heart beating, hard and heavy and wanting her.

"Why don't you come up here, you and Harvey? Stay at my apartment for the weekend and I'll——"

"Please, Kent." She was breathless. "I—there's something I want to talk to you about."

Fate. Angela in his dreams, messing up his days too. There had never been a woman before who got between him and his work. Sometimes lately he'd wondered if her image in his mind wasn't more real than the papers and the land and the money.

Seduction might not be enough. He knew that now, because half the time it wasn't even her touch that haunted him, but a yearning for the sound of her voice, the sight of the half angry, half laughing light in her eyes when she disagreed with him. The way the world seemed warmer, brighter, when he was near her.

Taking chances with money, with property, was something he did as a matter of course. Taking chances with relationships was different, frightening. He'd never had a relationship that qualified as risky.

Angela was not even surprised when Charlotte told her Kent was coming. She had overhead Harvey telling his new wife that it was time Kent was told the truth.

"I'm telling him," said Charlotte now. "Harvey thinks I've got to, and..."

Angela nodded. "It'll be a relief, won't it? Getting it out in the open? It won't be hanging over your head any more."

Charlotte threw back her short gray hair, spun around and paced to the living-room window. "How the hell do you tell your baby brother he's actually your son? When it's someone like Kent?'' She swung back and glared at Angela. ''This may sound crazy, but sometimes I feel I'm the younger one. He's always been so damned responsible, he'd never do any of the stupid things I've done in my life. He can be so——'' she sighed and her face looked bleak, older than her fifty-one years ''—so damned cold.''

Harvey was upstairs, showering. In a few minutes he would be taking his wife out to a live production of *A Midsummer Night's Dream*.

Angela went to Charlotte, touched her arm. ''I don't think you see Kent very clearly. All that coolness is just protective covering. He's not as invincible as you think.''

Charlotte's laugh was brittle. ''You don't know him!''

This weekend. Kent coming. Angela had a sail-cover order to finish or she would skip out to Seattle. Perhaps she could go over to Sally's, help with the baby, avoid Kent except when there were other people around. Maybe she would take Jake out fishing.

On Friday night, Angela saw his Chrysler when she came home from the shop, parked in the driveway. She parked beside him, knowing she had hoped he would turn up in a rental car, evidence that he had brought the jet down, that he would be leaving as abruptly as he came.

Inside, she found them all in the living room, Charlotte and Harvey sitting together on the sofa, Kent in the big chair where she had lain with him in the darkness that night.

He saw Angela first. She felt her motions go jerky. She stopped, standing behind the sofa, hanging on to it.

Charlotte twisted around and announced, ''Charles called. He wants you to call him back.''

Charles had been leaving messages for her on a daily basis, ever since the night she had been foolish enough to go to the theater with him. As a defense against Kent, Charles had proved worse than useless.

Charlotte added, "He said call as soon as you get in."

"I'll call him tomorrow." Kent was watching. That night, Kent's voice in the dark demanding to know why she had gone out with Charles. He had known why, even before she confessed the reason.

She said brightly, "Hello, Kent. How are you?" She thought she did that very well, her voice casual. He was a relative now, an in-law. She had to deal with him.

"Angela." His voice was casual too. He'd probably had time to decide she wasn't worth the hassle, and that was a good thing.

Wasn't it?

Harvey was pouring her a glass of the soda she liked, adding a twist of lemon. She took it from him with a smile. "Thanks, Dad. I'm going up for a shower."

"Going out tonight?" asked Kent.

"Yes." None of your business, her eyes told him. She glanced from his blue eyes to Charlotte's. One could hardly miss the resemblance between them, but Charlotte had not said her piece yet. Saturday, she had told Angela earlier. Poor Charlotte, she looked scared silly, although she was doing a fair job of hiding her nervousness, and Harvey was helping too. As Angela came in, she had overheard Harvey telling Kent about some property for sale south of town, offering to show him later. Talking real estate.

Angela felt guilty about her plans to avoid them all this weekend; but after all Charlotte had Harvey, and Harvey seemed endlessly willing to reassure his new wife, to stand by her and protect her. Angela would have found a relationship like that stifling, but it seemed to suit Charlotte. She seemed a new woman ever since she had come back from Mexico with Harvey, most of the restlessness gone, her smile quieter.

Angela didn't tell anyone that she was going to spend the evening with Sally, keeping her company while Barney was out working on a welding job. Better if Kent thought it was a date. Except that, later, she would make sure there was no meeting, no Kent and Angela alone together in the darkness of the night.

At Sally's house, they made pizza for supper. Jake helped, scattering cheese over everything and spilling the tomato sauce onto the floor. Later, they sat in the living room with the pizza on the coffee table and an old movie on the television. Sally and Angela watched the movie and Jake played with a Lego construction set. Angela changed baby Wendy when she cried, then gave her to Sally to feed.

All evening, she was aware that Kent was back at the house. She would not let herself wonder if he was waiting for her, but she could not shake the feeling that he was lying in the back of her mind.

Angela left about nine-thirty, knowing that Charlotte and Harvey would not have gone to bed yet. It worked out exactly as she had hoped. They were all together in the kitchen, drinking decaffeinated coffee and eating a batch of cinnamon buns. Charlotte was telling Kent about her difficulties with a taxi driver in Cabo San Lucas, Harvey was prompting her through the story and Kent was laughing.

"Have one of these?" offered Charlotte when Angela came into the kitchen.

"They're great," said Kent. He looked relaxed. She remembered McDonald's, that same look on his face as he talked about books and movies. "The coffee's good too," he added, smiling.

Angela's fingers curled in on themselves, fighting an urge to reach out and smooth back the stray lock of hair on his forehead. "Charlotte makes great coffee. I'm stuffed, though. Sally made pizza and Jake and I cleaned it up."

Harvey looked up. "I didn't know you were going to Sally's. I thought it was the latest boyfriend—Sam, isn't it?"

"Saul," she corrected. Kent was watching her, listening. "But I don't expect I'll be going out with him again."

"One more down the drain," teased Harvey, rolling his eyes toward Kent. "They never last long."

Angela flushed.

Kent tore off another bun and held it, turning it back and forth as if contemplating where to start eating. "Doesn't Saul measure up?"

She shrugged. "He's a psychologist. Every time I open my mouth, he tells me what I really meant. When I told him I didn't like horror movies, he told me I was trying to suppress violent urges toward my customers, afraid to sublimate my anger in case I lost control and struck out at a customer with a chain saw."

"That's a nice image," said Charlotte, laughing. "Angie cutting loose down at the shop with a chain saw!"

Kent handed her a cinnamon roll. "I'll take you out to dinner tomorrow and you can say whatever comes into your head without fear."

She said on a rush, "I'm going to Sally's again tomorrow."

"Couldn't you just as easily do that another night?"

She could not look away from his eyes—trapped, caught by what was inside herself. She nodded mutely.

"Seven, then?"

"All right." She swallowed and realized that Charlotte and Harvey were both watching her as if she was behaving very strangely. She held out the roll he had given her. "I really can't eat this. I'm going to bed."

In her room, she closed the door tightly. What had she done? Why did it feel so inevitable? Couldn't she say a simple "no"? She bit her lip and told herself that a twenty-nine-year-old widow had a right to an affair. It was her own business, wasn't it, if she wanted to go out with him for a while? He was only a man. There was no reason why he should be any more dangerous than Charles or Saul or any of the others.

She jumped when the knock came on the door. "Who is it?"

"Charlotte."

She pulled on her nightgown. "Come on in."

Charlotte closed the door behind her, leaning against it. She was whispering, her eyes narrowed, watching Angela with faint concern. "Angie, about Kent... You— I wouldn't want you to think you had to go out with him because of me. I mean, Kent is——"

"A woman-eating tiger?" suggested Angela wryly.

"Lord, no!" Charlotte spread her hands helplessly. "More—well, he's the same in all his relations. With Mom, with me, or with a woman. Kind of distant. Not— really not your type, Angie."

Distant? Oh, Lord! Angela felt the need to laugh hysterically. "Charlotte, it's just dinner. Don't worry."

Charlotte moved to the window, muttering, "What I'm worried about is telling him. He's going to hate me. Oh, Lord, Angie! He'll look at me as if I just crawled out from under a rock."

"Just explain to him how it was. He'll understand."

The older woman gulped. "Understanding was never very big in my family."

"He helped Harvey find you, didn't he? And he didn't react badly about your getting married?" Charlotte shook her head and Angela reminded her, "You thought he'd be scathing, but he wasn't."

Angela went to bed, lying in the dark, thinking about Kent's childhood. No wonder the people around him had seemed cold! Secrets being kept all around him. There would always be a strain to the relationships, the fear of the truth coming out.

Terribly difficult for Charlotte, of course, but in a way worse for Kent, because no one would ever explain the reason for the tension. And certainly the tension had been there. Charlotte had told Angela she had found it so difficult that she'd had to stay away from her home. She'd run into one disastrous relationship at the age of eighteen, trying to escape her parents, who had regarded her as a slut. Then she had got into a circle of friends who had too much money and too little to do, and she had wandered from party to party, almost homeless.

Charlotte had returned home when her son was in his teens, had wanted to tell him the truth at that point, but been persuaded not to by her mother. After her own father's death, years later, there had been another terrible argument between Charlotte and her mother. In the end, Charlotte had promised again to keep the secret.

Kent could not have been ignorant of the disputes, although he had never discovered the reason behind them. His home life had been stilted, without spontaneous love or laughter.

Angela woke early, dressed in jeans and a canvas shirt with green trim. The green brought out the color in her own eyes. She normally wore plain gold studs in her ears, but this morning she changed them for a pair of mother-of-pearl earrings that Barney and Sally had given her last Christmas. The mother-of-pearl was arranged to look like the wings of a butterfly.

She reached for the matching necklace, but decided that would be too obvious. She was probably crazy, dressing for a casual Saturday, adding jewelry, thinking of Kent.

She put on mascara to darken her lashes, added a coral lipstick and made a face at herself.

"You're looking for trouble, lady."

The girl in the mirror shrugged. Kent was going to haunt her until she got him out of her system. If she went out with him, maybe she would find that he was like all the other men she had dated since Ben's death— nice enough at first, but quickly developing feet of clay and irritating habits.

He was in the kitchen alone, standing in front of the coffee maker holding a glass carafe filled with water.

"Rescue me," he begged with a wry smile. "I can't figure out where the water goes." His hair was still damp from his shower, dark with wetness, just beginning to wave.

"There's a plastic reservoir for it." She reached in front of him and unlatched it, pulling it out. "Do you want me to do it?" She realized that she was leaning slightly toward him, wanting him to touch her, pull her close. She moved away jerkily.

"I'll do the water, but maybe you'd better put the coffee grounds in. I haven't a clue how much." She felt a jolt of sensation as he took the reservoir away from her. She froze, staring at the short pale line on the back of his thumb—a scar. She wanted to ask him what had happened, but knew her voice would be shaken and trembling. She grabbed the canister and started measuring coffee.

When they had the coffee started, she went to the refrigerator to get out eggs and milk. "Do you want an omelet?" she asked, thankful that her voice sounded almost normal.

He smiled. He had a shattering smile. "Sounds good. Can I do something?"

"Make toast," she suggested. "Bread's in the bread box, butter in the fridge. Do you cook your own meals at home?"

"Sometimes, when I'm staying in my apartment." That surprised her. She hadn't expected he would have any familiarity with kitchens and cooking. "Otherwise, when I'm at my mother's, there's a housekeeper who looks after all that. She's likely to throw a screaming fit and resign if anyone interferes in the kitchen."

"Sounds horrible." She frowned, picturing him as a boy, moving quietly through a house that didn't have enough love. "My home was like that, when I was a kid. But when I was fifteen Barney brought me home and I met Anna, Harvey's wife. This became my second home."

"You used to date Barney?"

She laughed. "More like sharing homework assignments and grousing about teachers together!"

"You grew up here? In Port Townsend?"

"Mmm." She pointed toward the side window. "Two blocks that way—a big, elegant house. Barney and I started kindergarten the same day. But I was a girl, so he ignored me."

"Your parents——"

"They live in England now. What was it like when you were a boy? Did you get to steal treats out of the fridge?"

"Only if I felt like living very dangerously." He took two pieces of toast out of the toaster as they popped. "Where's the butter? Tell me how the Sailing Rag business is going."

"It's developing." She handed him the butter, then went back to tend the first omelet. "I sent off a new lot of stuff to a store in Seattle that sells for me. Pants to match the shirts, and I'm working on designs for appliqués to put on the shirts. It's getting a bit much, though."

He slid two more slices of bread into the toaster. "In what way?"

"Too much work. I'm getting orders for more than I can produce." Last week she had spent every evening in the shop, working on filling a big order for the Seattle shop. "I'm getting behind in my other work."

He brought the plate of toast to the table. "Should we do some for Charlotte and Harvey? No? Then this is ready. Where's the cutlery?" She pointed and he got out knives and forks. "You could hire someone to help, free yourself for more design and promotion. It seems to me that if you're selling that much just out of your shop, and that Seattle sportswear place, you could expand pretty easily."

She slipped the second omelet out of the pan and sat down across from him. "I know a woman who would be good. She's a very meticulous seamstress, and she could do the Sailing Rags from the patterns I've made. But it's not that simple. I'd need more equipment—at the very least, another commercial sewing machine like the Conserve I've got downstairs." She frowned. "And another surger. A separate cutting table, because I'd have to have a place where she could cut when I'm working on a sail cover or a dodger." She shrugged. "It gets complicated. Expensive."

"If you've got the market, the investment should pay."

She covered a piece of toast with marmalade and admitted, "I don't have the money."

He frowned. "Why don't I send one of my accountants down to go over it with you, and we can work something out?"

"Work something out?" She shoved a piece of omelet around to the back of her plate. "Are you talking about loaning me money? I thought real estate was your territory."

"And investments. I think you'd be a good investment." He picked up his cup and his eyes were as businesslike as his voice.

"Me? Or Sailing Rags?" She did not want him to answer that, and added hurriedly, "I don't want to borrow money. It may take longer the way I'm doing it, but I'll get there without owing anyone a cent."

He shrugged. "The offer's open if you change your mind."

She wondered what was going to happen. Dinner tonight, and heaven knew where that would lead. No, she knew exactly where it was going. They would have an affair, and afterwards would be misery. Afterward... she might go away for a while. Get that seamstress in to take her place and go somewhere for the holiday Harvey kept saying she needed.

"What are your plans for this morning, Angela?"

She looked up from her plate. He was watching her, his eyes on the mess she was making of her omelet. "Are you going out somewhere? Running away again?"

She sighed. "Running away from you hasn't done me much good so far."

He smiled. "Are you going to work? At the shop?"

"No. I've got the seamstress I told you about in to look after the store today. Barney's taking the day off, taking Sally and the kids to Seattle for some shopping, so I thought I'd have a rest too. It's been a busy week."

"Spend the day with me." He was not smiling.

She mutilated what was left of the omelet.

"Angela?"

"I—Charlotte wants to talk to you this morning. I'm going to be out in the garage—the junk room upstairs in the old carriage house. I'm cleaning it out."

He shook his head, his eyes holding hers. "My sister can talk to me any time. I'll help you with the——"

"It's filthy—you'd hate it. Besides, you've got to give Charlotte time to—she's got something to tell you." She picked up her fork, dangling a piece of omelet. "It's hard for her, so will you be understanding?"

He dropped his knife on to his plate. "So there is a motive behind this weekend invitation." He looked grim. "What does she want?"

"She doesn't *want* anything." Angela pushed her plate away abruptly. "She—she's kind of scared of you, and she wants to...to tell you about something, and it's hard for her."

He leaned forward and took the fork out of her hand. "Do you know what it is?"

"Yes."

"Do you think she has reason to be afraid?"

She touched his hand. "You can be a very understanding man when you want to be."

He shook his head. "Don't you know I'm the original coldhearted bastard? I have it on the authority of at least two of the women in my life—you, and Charlotte."

Was she really one of the women in his life? Her lips parted, then she pressed them closed. "If I said that to you, I—I have a hot temper. You shouldn't listen." She flushed. The women in his life. She took the fork away from him, picked up her plate and headed for the sink with it, throwing back, "Then why don't you show us both that we're wrong? Starting with Charlotte this morning."

"Are you so sure you're wrong?"

She started the water running in the sink. She could feel him close behind her, could even smell the faintly soapy scent from his shower. She had lain in her bed earlier, listening to the sound of the shower, caught in a disturbing fantasy of Kent with the water streaming over his naked body.

"Yes, I'm sure I'm wrong." The coolness, the indifference he sometimes feigned was just a mask. He was a passionate man. It was the very intensity she sensed in him that frightened her when she thought of letting herself get caught up in him.

When she turned back to him, he had a faintly bemused expression in his eyes. She said quietly, "And you do have Charlotte's eyes."

"You've got a good imagination. Are you really going out to dinner with me tonight?"

She nodded. She was not going to fight what she felt for him any longer.

He caught her chin with one hand. She stared at him with eyes wide as his lips came to hers. He brushed his mouth softly on hers, taking her upper lip in a soft, sensual exploration. She could hear her own breathing when he lifted his head. Somewhere in that shattering exploration her eyes had closed. She dragged them open to find him watching her, his own eyes hiding nothing of what he wanted.

She stepped back, came against the counter. "I think you're probably the most dangerous thing I've run across in years." Ever.

He did not stop her when she went out to the garage.

She turned the light on in the room that had probably been quarters for the carriage driver in Victorian times. It was a mess in here, boxes stacked up without any labels to tell her what was inside. She wasn't sure when she had decided to attack it, or why, but three days ago she had asked Harvey if she could clear it out and turn this room into an apartment for herself.

"Angie, you don't have to move out," he had protested. "There's lots of room in this house."

She had hugged him quickly, reassuring him. "I know that, Dad. But why shouldn't you and Charlotte have some privacy? And I've been thinking about a place of my own."

Kent coming, and if Charlotte had her way he would come again and again, visiting. Angela thought he would come, because he had seemed to be enjoying himself last night, relaxed in the kitchen. And this morning.

So if she wanted to avoid Kent, it might make sense for her to find her own place. That was what she had been thinking by Friday. But then he had asked her to dinner, and she had undone all her good resolutions by accepting. When had she decided that she was going to go out with him? The decision seemed to have been made for her in some part of her subconscious.

She pulled out a box, wondering if she had any hold on her thoughts, her actions at all. Maybe this clean-up business was a plan of her subconscious, to give herself living quarters where it would not be noticed if Kent came to her in the night.

Her heart was racing, her thoughts too graphic for comfort. She pulled open the box and found it filled with children's toys. These must have been Barney's and Ben's when they were small—building blocks, part of a train set. Harvey would probably want them to go to his grandchildren, Jake and the baby Wendy.

The next box was toys too, and she started a pile along an empty bit of wall for Barney and Sally. Then clothes. She hadn't realized Anna was so sentimental, but she seemed to have kept every article of clothing her children had ever worn. These baby clothes might be good for Wendy. The other things—styles had changed so much since Anna's children were small that Angela doubted much of this would be any use. She didn't think Harvey was going to keep much of it, but maybe Barney would want it. Not likely, though, Barney really wasn't the sentimental type.

She heard the footsteps on the stairs. She knew it was Kent. He moved more quickly than Harvey, with more purpose. His step was heavier than Charlotte's. Angela sat cross-legged on the floor, waiting.

He stopped in the doorway, looking around, taking it in. He pushed one hand into his pant pocket, a sign that he was disturbed. "What's all this?" His voice was ironic, the same cold tones he had used the first time she saw him. He had his mask on.

Angela waved at the box in front of her crossed legs. "I'm clearing up, deciding what to throw and what to keep."

"What is it?" He sounded as if he had never seen a junk room before. "Looks like the inside of one of those thrift shops."

"That's where a lot of this will go. It's all the things Anna stowed away over the years."

"Doesn't Harvey want to——?"

She laughed. "He doesn't want to be bothered with it. I thought I'd clear this out, make a place for myself here." He was looking at her oddly and she flushed, remembering her own thoughts about her possible motives. "Charlotte and Harvey," she added quickly. "They should be more to themselves, not have an old daughter-in-law hanging around."

He looked back, through the window that faced the house. "Come out with me, Angela."

"I told you I would." She frowned, seeing the tension in his face. "Dinner tonight, remember?"

"I mean now." He crossed the littered floor quickly and caught her wrist. "Come on."

"Where?" Her wrist was burning where he touched, but for once his touch on her was almost rough, not seductive or gentle.

"Out. For a drive." He shook his head, obviously rattled. "I don't know—somewhere. Just come, for heaven's sake! I—damn it, I just have to get out of here! If I storm out alone, Charlotte's going to think I'm upset."

She came to her feet too quickly, her hands pressing against his chest. "Charlotte told you?"

"Yeah." He shrugged. "Come on, will you? I need you."

He did not mean that, not the way it sounded. She looked at his face and decided. "All right. Will you let me drive that car of yours?"

"What the hell. Why not?" He laughed shortly.

She moved away from him suddenly. "No, Kent, you can't take off—not now. Of course you're upset. Why shouldn't you be?"

"You know all about this?" He was trying that cold voice, but it didn't fool her.

"Yes. She told me, before I ever met you. And if you go out now, she'll think you're rejecting her."

"Rejecting *her*?" He swung around, but the floor was so cluttered, there was nowhere to pace. "She's the one who rejected me!"

Angela moved to him, touched his chest again. "That's a pretty harsh judgment of a fifteen-year-old girl. Did you tell her that?" Poor Charlotte, scared stiff, and Kent shutting his feeling inside, that harsh look on his face.

"No, of course I didn't." She felt his chest expanding with tension. "I was trying to take it in, and you've no idea how difficult it is. Charlotte's such a scattered, irresponsible person. I've always felt older than her. How the hell can she be my mother?"

She put her hands on his arms, stilling his restless movements. "Try to understand her. I know it's a shock, finding out your sister is really your mother, but despite—she always hated the deception of it. Your

mother—grandmother, I mean—would never let her tell
you, and...for Charlotte, I think it was always easier
to run away than face up to unpleasantness.''

''Yeah.'' He closed his eyes. He looked tired.

''Are you angry?''

He sighed and grimaced wryly. ''How the hell can
anyone stay angry at her?''

''No.'' Angela smiled. ''She's a charmer, isn't she?''
So was her son, except Kent had all the strengths his
mother was lacking. ''Did she tell you how it happened,
who your father was?''

''Someone she was dating.''

She could feel the muscles of his upper arms hard
under her hands. She thought he should know, and said
quietly, ''A boy she was dating. She was in love, young
and...well, she was very young. Her parents didn't like
the boy much. She used to say she was going to a girlfriend's. Just fifteen, and she didn't know anything
about protecting herself. Afterward—well, when she
found out she was pregnant, by then they'd broken up
and he was taking out another girl.''

He cursed, then said grimly, ''What did she do?''

''She was afraid to tell anyone.''

He closed his eyes tightly. ''I don't wonder! My
parents—my grandparents, that is—were not understanding people.'' He moved away from her touch,
pacing through the litter to the window, then back. ''And
Charlotte—well, she would have put off telling she was
pregnant as long as she could. When she did——'' He
closed his eyes again. ''Poor Charlotte! My mo—my
grandmother would have torn her up. That's one lady
who has no room for human failing.''

Angela relaxed a little, feeling the tension leaving him.
''Why don't you give me a hand with this mess?''

Kent peered into the box she had just opened. ''I can
think of things I'd rather do.''

"It's therapeutic."

He laughed and picked out a book from the box. "This one sounds like a real thriller. What are we sorting them into? Knowing you, this apparent chaos will have some sort of order."

"That pile over there is for the thrift store. That one's for Barney. The other two are Harvey—and throw away."

"Do either Harvey or Barney like thrillers?"

She shook her head. "Sailing books for Harvey, though."

He dropped the book into the thrift-shop pile. He went through six or seven more books, asking her about most of them. Then he said quietly, "Harvey's son was your husband. Some of this was his, I'd imagine."

Ben. He might as well be a stranger who had died. She sighed. "Put that one in Barney's pile—he's a Sherlock Holmes fan. Those cowboy ones you can turf in the shop pile. Nobody in the family reads them."

"Were they your husband's?"

She nodded. "Ben would have liked to have been born back when gunslingers roamed from town to town, having adventures and riding off into the sunset."

Kent turned back from putting three cowboy books on the growing pile. Angela shrugged away the curiosity in his eyes. "My husband was good at riding off into the sunset. He didn't like responsibilities. That one—the next in that pile—is an old cookbook. Put it aside for Charlotte, she might want to try out some of the recipes."

He put it where she indicated, then worked his way through several more cowboy adventures. "I was surprised to see that Charlotte can cook. I've never seen her in a kitchen."

"She took a course in Paris once."

"You know more about her than her own family does. Do people just naturally confide in you, Angela?"

"Not particularly."

"Yes," he said softly. "Yes, particularly. Jake asks you intimate questions about where babies come from, customers come in and share their problems, and Charlotte tells you her life's secrets and I..."

She smiled. "You don't tell me a lot."

"More than I tell anyone else." He shrugged and hurriedly picked up a handful of books. "What do you do with school texts?"

"Thrift shop. Sally's not going to want that lot. They'd fall apart if Jake touched them."

They worked together in silence for what seemed a long time. It was a comfortable silence. Angela looked up once and saw that Kent's immaculate shirt was covered with smears of dust. She hid a smile and bent to the box.

From downstairs came Charlotte's voice. "Angie? Are you up there?"

"Yes!" she called back. "I've roped Kent in, and we're sorting our way through utter chaos."

"Oh! I——" Silence. Then, "Do you two want something to drink?"

Angela looked at Kent pointedly. He knew what she wanted him to do, and called down, "Something long and cold with ice would be lovely!"

"I'll get it." Charlotte's voice sounded lighter now.

Kent pulled another box over and started opening it. "What are you smirking about?"

She wanted to go into his arms, to hug him close. Instead, she stared at his hands and said unsteadily, "That you're a failure as a coldhearted bastard."

"Hmm." His lips twitched. "Is that why you're going out with me tonight?"

"Maybe."

"A noncommittal answer? That's not like you, Angela. Blunt and to the point is more like it. That's one of the things that fascinates me about you."

Fascinates? She dropped her eyes, confused. "If this is all decorations, let's pack it back up and put it in Barney's pile." She pulled a tangled mess of Christmas tree lights out of the new box. "Harvey's got all the decorations he needs in the basement."

They dug through the box, took out two regular light bulbs and an extension cord, then repacked it. Then Kent sucked in a deep breath and said, "I think I'd better go down and talk to her."

She nodded, but before he got up he leaned across and slid his fingers into her hair. "Did you know you've got a big dust smear right here?" He kissed the tip of her nose.

She rubbed her nose with the back of her hand. She knew she was smiling, could not seem to stop her response to him. "Shall I start listing your dusty spots?"

"No, just give me a kiss, for luck."

"You'll do fine. Just remember that she's scared too, and it'll be okay."

His nervousness showed in his eyes. "Maybe, but this isn't the kind of talking I'm accustomed to, so give me the kiss anyway. I need it."

She kissed him quickly on the lips.

"You can do better than that." His voice was husky.

Her heart was trying to smash its way through her rib cage. "Not this time," she whispered.

"Maybe not," he agreed, his eyes crinkling although his lips were not smiling. "A real kiss from you is more intimate than making love to other women. I might not make it down the stairs."

He turned and left her without waiting for an answer. A good thing, because her heart was thundering and she might have said something really crazy. She heard him whistling tunelessly as he ran down the stairs. She stared at her dusty hands. It was worse than she had imagined. The sexual attraction was shattering enough, way out of her experience, but she was starting to like him—too much. Her crazy mind was whispering about loving, but, no matter how nice he turned out to be under that mask he tried to wear, he was not a man for forever. She had to remember that.

She was deranged if she thought she could have an affair with him and walk away whole. He wasn't Charles or Saul, and it was all too easy to see herself begging him to love her, to take her forever. She gritted her teeth, stared at the mess around her, then closed her eyes tightly and remembered Kent outside her door, telling her not to worry because he was not looking for permanence.

CHAPTER SEVEN

KENT unlocked the driver's door, turned and asked with a grin, "Do you want to drive it?"

Intimacies. Touching his arm. Watching the creases that formed at the corners of his eyes when he was amused. Driving his car.

"No." Angela moved away from him, to the passenger door. "If I smashed it up, you'd probably kill me."

"You wouldn't smash it." He stared at her across the roof of his car, sensing something of what she was thinking. Abruptly, he got in and opened the door for her. "Anyway, it's insured." He started the engine. It was very quiet.

She hugged herself, sitting in the passenger seat, feeling the air from the heater changing from cool to warm, blowing on her legs through her nylons.

He put the car into gear, twisted around to reverse. His hand brushed her shoulder and she jerked. She felt like a seventeen-year-old. She tried to remember being seventeen, dating Barney, then Ben coming back from wherever he'd been off working. She hadn't been scared then, she realized. Excited, probably because she had been too young, too stupid to know the risks.

"What's wrong?"

She stared ahead. There was a woman crossing at the crossroads, and Kent stopped for her. The woman gave Kent a quick grin and a wave of thanks.

"I think this is a bad idea."

The car started. She stared at her hands, at the faint depression where Ben's ring had been. She had taken the

ring off before she went to the doctor. Ben was gone.
Wearing his ring when she was thinking about having
an affair seemed wrong to her.

"What's a bad idea?" he asked quietly. "Dinner?"

She sighed. "You know what I mean."

She glanced at him, saw his mouth a hard line. A
muscle in his jaw clenched and he turned left instead of
right, driving through the houses on the outskirts of Port
Townsend.

"Where are we going?" she asked.

He could take her anywhere. She had no defenses.
She knew she could not fight him, that it would not even
come to that. All he had to do was look at her and she
would be lost in his eyes. Damn it! He didn't even have
to touch her!

She chewed her lip, staring through the windshield,
knowing she had never behaved like such a fool in all
her life. Dinner, and that tension building, and knowing
all the time where it was going. Kent would make love
to her, and she would lose control completely. When he
left, she might be crazy enough to chase after him. It
could end with her calling his office day after day,
begging him to come back to her. And that was insane
too, because she did not want forever from him. His life-
style was the last thing she needed, money and being
nice to the right people.

Oh, God! Now she was thinking about marriage! With
Kent. She gulped and blinked. There must be books on
how to handle an affair, but she'd never read one and
she knew she was going to make a mess of it.

He stopped in a half-empty parking lot. Point Wilson.
She stared through the windshield at the lighthouse, the
beach.

When he opened the door she got out. She had to
make some kind of conversation. Maybe she could just

talk her way through this evening. If she got through it intact, she would . . .

She looked around. There were two women walking out toward the point. Other than that, they were alone.

"There's nowhere to eat here," she pointed out.

"No," he said grimly. "I figured if I drove far enough, I'd find somewhere we could be alone."

Alone. She shoved her hands into her pockets. "This is Point Wilson. Ben used to bring me out here."

He muttered something under his breath, then took her arm. "I suppose this is the local lovers' lane. Come on, let's take a walk."

Daylight still, although the sun was low in the sky. She went with him over the dunes toward the beach. They walked in silence, slowly, looking out over the wild water around the point. When they stopped, there was just white water ahead and Kent at her side. She had not looked at him the whole time. What would he say if she said something like, "Let's go to a motel?" Maybe that really was the answer. Just get it over quickly, and it might not touch her so much.

"The tidal current is terrible off this point." She pushed her free hand deep into the pocket of her coat. He had her other hand tucked firmly under his arm and she kept fighting the urge to curl her fingers into his forearm, to hold on.

He turned to face her, taking her hand in his, staring down at it. "You're not wearing his ring any more."

"No," she whispered.

"Then . . ." He sighed. "Angela, this is insane."

"I know," she agreed miserably. What man would want an idiot? "Why don't you . . . why don't you just—just forget about it?"

He was turning her hand in his, playing with her fingers. She could feel his touch all the way up her arm.

If he didn't stop, she was going to scream. Maybe screaming was exactly the thing she should do.

"Just go away and forget you?" His voice was strained.

"Yes. I—don't you think it would be the best thing?" She could feel the pain in her chest. Oh, God, maybe it was already too late! He was going to be in her dreams forever and she would wake in the night crying for him.

He shook his head as he stroked her palm with his thumb. "Best, maybe. But it doesn't work. I've already tried it."

"Well, if——" She gulped. "You're only here this weekend because Charlotte called you."

He laughed shortly. "If she hadn't called, I might have lasted another six or seven days. Damn it, Angela, do you realize what I did last week? I——"

"What?"

He shook his head. He had been dictating a letter to Patricia, an offer for a property on one of the Gulf Islands, and Angela's name had come out in the middle of a sentence about terms. Patricia had stared at him and he hadn't even realized for a minute what he'd said.

He dropped her hand and pushed his hands into his pockets and said angrily, "Give me one good reason why you won't go out with me!" He jerked his hand out of his pocket in a frustrated gesture. "I don't believe I said that. I sound like a ten-year-old. Damn it, Angela, you're turning my brain to sawdust!"

He swung away, glaring at the white water. Hell, he was making a mess of this. When he turned back, she was staring at him, looking half scared to death, as if his shouting had made her expect he would strike her next.

"Angela, why do you fight it?" He touched her arm. "If you can go with the lukewarm Charles, why not——?" She jerked away, her jaw set. Where the hell was his ability to negotiate? He spread his hands in a placating gesture. "Angela, I find you very attractive and...and you're not indifferent to me. Hell, I'll even keep my hands off you if that's what you want." He crammed his fists into his pockets. "What can you lose, Angela? A few dinners. The theater."

She was staring at a point below his chin. He growled angrily, "What makes me so much more impossible than Charles, for God's sake?"

"Charles and I didn't make love."

The words didn't make sense to him at first, then suddenly he understood. He touched her face, and she shivered. Her skin was soft and smooth and she would not look up at his eyes. He remembered the feel of her in his arms, his lips finding places that were so soft, trembling. The fire in her eyes and on her flesh.

"Angela, are you telling me that you went out with Charles for months, and you didn't...?"

She flushed at the knowledge in his eyes. He was so close she could feel his body heat.

"How long since your husband died?"

"Seven years," she whispered.

"And there's been no one?" He closed his eyes and she saw him swallow. "God, that's like going out with a virgin. Why not, Angela? Are you afraid of making love?"

She shook her head. "I just—I didn't want to. There was nobody that I——"

"You wanted me." He laughed, an uncomfortable sound. "Almost a year with Charles, and how many other boyfriends?" She shook her head and he said, "If you were going out with me, I wouldn't give us a week before——"

She whispered, "I know."

His eyes found hers. "Scared, Angela?"

"Yes." There was no point in denying it. She was terrified of what he did to her.

"I would never hurt you."

She shivered. "Not physically, I know that, but—but emotionally—I think you'd tear me into pieces." She tied her fingers together into knots and muttered, "I'm not willing to risk that."

He turned away. She hugged herself and watched him walk along the beach toward the Point. Away from her. If she had been looking for words to send him away, she seemed to have found them at last.

She loved him. Senseless though it was, she was in love with Kent—suddenly, violently, hopelessly. Not soft, young passion, not dreams and hopes. This was different—more, it was harsh and all-consuming, and it was going to tear her up for a long time. Years of looking at Charlotte, trying not to ask when Kent would be visiting next, hanging around and knowing it was hopeless, but unable to leave.

She was hopeless at any kind of pretense. He would know.

She got into the car and stared through the windshield, glad it faced the trees and not the beach, that she didn't have to watch him. She heard him walking across the asphalt of the parking lot.

He opened the driver's door and got in. She saw his fingers curl around the steering wheel. She said dully, "You don't have to take me to dinner. Just take me back home."

She heard the breath he took in, deep and ragged. He probably had an urge to slap her. His kind of affair had rules, and she was not playing by the rules.

He stared at the trees, that muscle in his jaw twitching every few seconds. Finally he said tonelessly, "We could get married."

She shivered and her voice was sharp and high. "Please don't do that!"

His chest swelled and she thought he was going to explode. Cold Kent—but he wasn't. He was white-hot under the repressions. She wasn't sure exactly what emotion he was hiding under that toneless proposal, but she was not insane enough to accept. She hugged herself tighter.

"I'll go away with you if you want. I—it's not that I'm putting the price on myself——" She squeezed her eyes closed.

He turned the key and the Chrysler's engine came to life with a subdued roar.

She said painfully, "You don't want to get married."

"Probably not," he agreed without expression. "But your reaction is hardly flattering. Is there some reason why the idea of marriage made you scream?"

"I didn't scream." The car was getting warmer now. She undid the buttons on her coat, then did them up again.

"You did, and you've been shivering ever since. Can't you put anyone in your husband's place, Angela?"

"It isn't that."

"You loved him."

"Yes." She deliberately unwrapped her arms and tangled her hands together in her lap. "The whole thing was doomed from the start."

"Are you talking about us? Or your marriage?"

Oh, God! She gripped her hands together more tightly. "Both, I guess. I was a pretty stupid kid."

He took her hands and held them between his. "Tell me."

"It's not exciting. I was seventeen. It was spring, and I was going to graduate in a couple of months... My parents had my future all worked out—college, then a year in Europe, then some man my father would approve of. My father was a doctor. My mother was from what she liked to call an important family."

"Your parents were living here then?"

"Yes." She shifted and looked away from him, at the dark sky. "They're in England now. It's been a long time since I've seen them. They write and I answer, but we don't have much in common and they're so far away." She turned her hand and his fingers threaded through hers. "Ben. Well, I was dating Barney, you see. We'd always been in the same class, and we'd dated off and on through high school." She shrugged. "If I'd had a brother, I'd have wanted him to be like Barney. Part of the charm was his home too, you see—Harvey and Anna. Anna taught me to cook."

He stroked the back of her hand. "Where did Ben come in?"

"I'd never seen much of him until—he was four years older, and he'd gone off to take his welding, then one job and another." She wasn't doing a very good job of getting to the point. She twisted her hand in his, but he wasn't letting go. "He came back that spring."

"And you fell in love?"

"He was ... exciting, I guess. Older. He made me feel very grown up, very attractive. That was exciting too. My mother didn't like him at all, and my father forbade me to go out with him."

He shifted a little, turning to see her better. He brushed a curl back behind her ears. "You went out with him anyway?"

"I'd never been in love before. I'd never even been out here before, until Ben brought me."

She stared at his hand on hers. Her skin was tanned almost as darkly as his. "I wasn't experienced at all. Barney knew that, I suppose, and he got mad at Ben. At the time I thought it was because Barney was jealous, but I think it was just that he was worried Ben might take advantage. Barney got his nose broken. Poor Barney, and I was young and silly enough that I thought it proved Ben really loved me. When Ben asked me to run away with him, I was scared, but he said we'd get married." She shrugged. "That was my price. I didn't think of it that way, of course, but I think Ben did. And although I wrote 'and they lived happily ever after' in my diary, I don't think it ever meant that much to Ben."

What was Kent thinking under the hard line of his lips, the eyelids that had dropped over his eyes to conceal their expression?

She tried again to get her hand away, said almost frantically, "So you see, I've had enough of getting married just because ... just because ..."

He touched her cheek, his voice whimsical. "You're amazing, Angela. So blunt, and then embarrassed at the strangest things."

She was already flushed. She gave up on tugging at her hand. "You're thinking I was a pretty stupid kid?"

"No." He half smiled. "Actually, I was thinking that when you were seventeen, running away to marry the man you'd fallen in love with, I would have been twenty-three."

"What were you doing when you were twenty-three?" She tried to picture him. He wouldn't have had those lines on his forehead, but the chin would still have had that stubborn certainty that it was right. Maybe he would have laughed a little more easily then, but she didn't think so.

"I'd just graduated—business admin, of course. I was working for my father. Serious business. What with that and—I'd decided that I was going to keep my mind on business, and no woman was ever going to make a fool of me." He grinned wryly. "Again, that was."

"What was her name?"

"Sophia."

"Was she pretty?"

He laughed. "Absolutely gorgeous, and equally greedy. She was also married, which she neglected to mention. Considering how quickly I got over her, I don't imagine you could say I was in love with her."

Had he ever been in love?

He brushed a curl away from her ear. "Are you going to tell me the rest?"

She shook her head.

"He was the fool, Angela, if he had you and didn't realize how much . . . how special you are."

She leaned across to give him a quick, soft kiss on his cheek. "Thank you."

He pushed the gearshift into drive, turned to reverse, then stopped with his arm along the back of the seat, staring at her. "Jake—when Jake asked why you and Uncle Ben hadn't had children—I saw your face. Angela, I—I have to know why you looked like that." The car started to crawl back and he pushed the brake, stopping it as he touched her face.

She cleared her throat and swallowed the tears that always wanted to overcome her when she thought of the baby. "I—I—you see, I was——" She jerked her head away from his touch. "Ben didn't want children. He made that clear at the beginning. He didn't want to be married either."

"Angela . . ." He jerked the shift lever into park again and took her face in both his hands. "Honey——"

"We were together five years, wandering around, chasing construction jobs. Then I got pregnant and he left me." She shrugged and admitted sadly, "I don't know when I stopped loving him. Maybe—maybe it was all dreams and wanting to be in love. It died somewhere, maybe then, when he left me alone. I—Anna and Harvey . . . they came and got me."

"Came? Where were you?"

"Upstate New York. A construction site again, living in the trailer, except—— I don't want to talk about this."

He massaged her jaw, slid his hands into her hair and stroked the tension in her. "It's inside you, bunched up, and it's affecting you and me."

She drew in a shaky breath that seemed to fill her lungs in jerky pieces. "After I told him . . . he didn't say anything. I—I—— The next day I went into town, shopping for groceries. I took the bus in. When I came back, he was gone. The trailer was gone, the truck. Just . . . everything."

Kent's fingers were digging into her scalp. He pulled them away when she made a sound of protest. "He left you alone in New York with nothing?"

"Yes. I knew he wouldn't come back. I'd seen his face when I told him about the baby. I—I found a job waiting tables, and a room to stay in." She could feel the anger in Kent. He wanted to strike out, to protect her, but it was so long ago. She touched his chest uneasily. "It's all past history. I can't really even remember his face now. I look at Barney, and I know Ben looked a lot like Barney, but I can't make the picture in my mind."

"You kept wearing his ring," said Kent with an effort. "Why the hell did you wear his ring when he did that to you?"

She looked away, bit her lip. "Protection, I guess. I didn't want to be dependent on anyone . . . ever again."

He covered her hand, holding it against his chest. "And the baby?"

She shook her head. "I'll cry if I talk about it. I don't want to cry."

He didn't say anything, just held her hand close against him. She gulped and said, "I—the shock, I guess. I ended up in the hospital and—and I had a miscarriage." She gulped and blinked. Her voice caught. "I—I didn't want to lose the baby. I'd always wanted...I called Anna. They came and got me, paid the hospital bill and drove me home.''

He touched her cheek, brushed at the dampness. She shuddered and he pulled her into his arms. Where the hell had her own parents been when she had needed them? And the bastard she had married?

She whispered, "Harvey and Anna—I think they hoped Ben would change, come back and—Harvey was looking for him, but I knew it was over. I knew I'd been fooling myself for a long time that it could work. The police contacted us a few weeks later. Ben had died in a freeway accident."

Kent closed his eyes tightly and held her close, feeling her tears against his neck and wishing he could have been there for her. Wanting to give her all the things she had believed she was getting when she wrote "and they lived happily ever after" in her diary. Children. Love. A home that was her own, forever.

He smoothed her curly head, felt her grow quiet in his arms. I love you. He had not even thought he knew what the words meant, but holding her, feeling her tears still damp on his neck, he knew that he wanted to share the rest of his life with her. Hold her in his arms when she was hurt, hear her laughter when she was happy. Feel her sleeping beside him in the night.

She pushed against his chest, and he let her go.

"I'm a mess," she muttered.

He found a tissue and gave it to her, said, "You're beautiful."

"I'm not." She scrubbed at her eyes with the Kleenex. "Pretty sometimes, when I put makeup on and——"

He said awkwardly, "I meant it about getting married."

She muttered, "You're too damned chivalrous. You can't marry someone just because you think they need looking after." She shook her head. "I wouldn't suit you at all. You need someone with more polish, and I—— If I ever got married again, it would have to be someone who wanted the same kind of life I want."

He wanted to ask her what she wanted, promise to give it to her, but it was the wrong time. Her eyes were swollen from her tears and she was working at smiling, trying to shake off the memories she had shared with him. He thought of her in the shop, patiently answering Jake's endless questions. So much love in her. He thought of her baby, wanted to give her his child, to see her looking down on their baby with tenderness and love in her eyes.

He cleared his throat. "Dinner, then?"

"All right," she whispered. "But stop at that building on the other side of the parking lot. I'll go in and splash cold water on my face."

Inside the ladies' room, Angela stared at her reflection, eyes red and swollen. That was a stupid way to turn down a proposal. Crying all over the man! He would be out there thinking what a lucky escape he had had. She ran cold water and slapped her face with it. Then she put her eye makeup back on and she looked a little less like a raccoon.

She brushed her hair and decided that she looked almost normal. She would stay that way too, damn it! No more crying all over him. He had felt sorry for her, and he was kind enough to try to reassure her. If she had said yes...

It was impossible. She could never fit into the world where he lived. In the middle of the city, in the midst of all that money. He didn't even live in the same country.

She brushed her hair again, then she went back to him.

Inside the car, there was soft music playing. She got in. It was almost dark now. Kent stared at her so oddly that she asked nervously, "Do I look all right?"

"Definitely. There's just one thing." He touched her ear. "Your butterfly is upside-down."

She made herself stay very still while he turned the butterfly earring. "It must be loose," she said shakily when his hand left her ear. She bent her head and pushed the back a little more tightly on to her ear.

He traced the line of her ear, half smiling. "I'm going to start looking at women's earrings. I want to buy you some that are gold and a little dangly. I'd like to see them lying against your skin here." He touched just under her ear. "Moving when you walk..."

"Kent..." She moistened her lips, not knowing what words she had meant to say. Just his voice could send her blood wild. "Where...where are we going for dinner?"

He smiled. "Somewhere we can dance. I want to dance with you."

She was glad he had to turn away to drive. Just the thought of dancing in his arms did violent things to her body.

"All right?" he asked.

She nodded, although she thought she might start trembling when he took her in his arms on the dance floor. Had a woman ever fainted from just feelings? Sensations, touching, wanting more.

When he stopped, she stared at the building. He bent over and kissed her parted lips lightly. "Stay right here. I'll only be a minute."

"McDonald's?"

"You'll see."

Then he was gone, inside the building. He emerged about three minutes later, carrying a paper bag. He put the bag in her lap. She could feel the warmth through her skirt.

"Take out?"

"That's right. A twenty-piece order of chicken nuggets. We can share, can't we?" She nodded numbly, suppressing the urge to giggle. The corners of his lips twitched and he said, "I thought I'd surprise you."

She let the giggle free. "Takeout doesn't go with the white Chrysler and the tailored suits. Did you change your mind about the dancing? Afraid I'd step on your toes?"

She didn't care what she ate, but she needed to be in his arms.

He turned right, up the hill and away from the town. She leaned back, the warmth from the bag in her lap, content to let him take her anywhere, not asking questions until he pulled off on to a small, lonely gravel road.

"What's down here?"

He was surprised. "Haven't you been out here before?"

"No." Her heart was beating in heavy thuds. "What— I thought you didn't know this area?"

"Harvey took me looking at real estate last night."

The road narrowed, then abruptly terminated in a wide grassy clearing surrounded by trees. Kent stopped the car and turned off both the engine and the headlights, leaving only the music from his car stereo. Soft music, dreamy music. Music for dancing with a lover.

He got out of the car and Angela saw him walk around the front of it, his body a dark silhouette in the moonlight. He opened her door and reached in for her hand.

"Dance with me?" His voice was husky. She put aside the bag of food and let him pull her up to her feet, into his arms. Here, away from the water, the night air was surprisingly warm. He slipped her coat off and dropped it back into the car.

"Do you mind?" he asked quietly.

She shook her head and moved to him.

There was no need for words. The ground was soft under their feet, the music only a breath on the night air, the moon only a gentle hint of light. He turned and brought her closer into his arms. She slipped both arms around his neck and turned her face into his shoulder, letting him take her weight, her body moving with his, feeling each slight shift as he moved slowly to the music.

When the music stopped, he slid his hand up into the hair at the back of her neck. She lifted her face away from his shoulder, let his hand take the weight of her head as she tipped it back to look up into his face.

He was staring down at her, his own eyes in shadow, her face glowing in the moonlight. He said, "I wanted to dance with you, hold you in my arms." She thought he smiled. His hand moved, her curls slipping through his fingers. Then he whispered, "But I didn't want anyone else. I wanted to be able to do this." He bent and covered her lips with his, brushing softly, then withdrawing.

It was a good thing he was holding her. Her eyes fell shut and she had no strength to hold herself up, especially when he murmured, "...and this," kissing the soft vulnerability of her closed eyelid, then moving to caress the other lid with his lips.

"Kent..."

"Hmm?" The music had started again, still slow and very soft. He guided her head to his shoulder and began to dance again, only now they were together so intimately that she could feel every hard muscle of his masculine body as he moved with her.

This time when the music stopped she opened her eyes and found that the car was behind him. He leaned against it, taking her with him. She gasped at the sudden, intimate contact and he bent to take her open mouth with his.

"See what you do to me," he groaned when he finally let her lips free. His hands slid along her back, molding the length of her to his own hard body. "I was insane enough to think I could bring you out here and we could dance and talk... and kiss a little... Oh, baby... kiss me."

She found his lips open, ready for her. There was nothing cool about him, from his harsh breathing to the heat of his neck as she slid her fingertips in an exploration along the ridges of his muscles.

When his lips moved from hers, she tipped back her head and he found the long line of her throat, the heated flesh above her bodice. "Did you wear this deliberately?" he asked hoarsely. It was the blouse she had worn the night she came home to find him waiting for her in the darkness.

"Yes." She remembered how her fingers had trembled as she tied the lace that held the blouse together so cleverly. "Yes," she whispered. "Are you going to seduce me?"

She saw him close his eyes, saw the shudder that went through his body, and felt it. She touched his neck, his face, slid her fingers down along the hard line of his throat and heard him groan her name.

"Angela... oh, baby, I want to..."

He lifted her in his arms, taking her swiftly to the softest place, where the grass grew thick under a big, overhanging tree. She stared up at him, hearing the harsh, shallow sound of his breathing, the soft music over it all. He touched her face and she reached up and caught his hand, drawing it lower to the warm swollen curve of her breast.

"I couldn't find the tie last time," she whispered. "I looked everywhere, but I couldn't find it. I had to make a new one."

He traced the line where the lacy blouse met soft flesh. "It was in my pocket. I've still got it . . . I kept it." He pulled the tie and she gasped as his fingers found the warm silkiness of her camisole. His fingers slid along the silky undergarment, seeking and finding the hard swelling. "Last time you were wearing a bra. I knew you weren't tonight. When you came down the stairs at the house, I could see you moving. And when . . . just knowing . . . wondering what you had on under that blouse . . . it's been driving me insane all night, watching you."

He pushed the blouse away and concentrated on the satiny feel of her curves through the camisole. When she groaned his name, he bent his lips to where his hands had been, kissing her through the camisole, then suddenly needing more, pushing the thin straps down and finding what he sought with his mouth.

He stroked her to a fever, his hands and his lips and the hard need of his body. When her hands worried at his shirt, he impatiently shed his jacket, pulling off his tie and shirt and throwing them aside too. Then he took her hand and held it against his chest so that she could feel the hard slamming of his heart.

"Feel that? Feel what you do to me?" He bent and licked the hard nipple of one breast slowly with his tongue, then demanded hoarsely, "You feel it too, don't you? You wore that seductive thing, with hardly anything underneath, because you knew what it would do to me, and you wanted——"

"Yes," she admitted. She had seen it from the beginning, the effect she had on him, making his eyes lose their coolness, his lips smile or frown or go hard with anger. "I wanted ... I was afraid of it, but I couldn't seem to stop myself wanting ... you."

She spread her hands over his chest, felt the hard heartbeat and his stillness. She knew it would end in a second, that he would bend to her again and there would be no more hesitation, nothing that could stop what was between them.

"I'll protect you, Angela."

She drew her fingers along the two ridges of muscle that led from his chest down to his hard midriff. "You don't have to. I went to the doctor a few weeks ago."

"Weeks?" He touched her face.

Her fingers curled around his belt buckle. "I was too susceptible to you to take any chances. I was planning to hold out, but I didn't have much faith in my powers of resistance." She smiled, teased softly, "What's stopping you now?"

He took her mouth first, then her warm woman's body in his arms. He started slowly, touching and kissing, finding the places that made her gasp, trembling himself when she groaned. Her hands were restless on him, needing desperately what he was holding back.

He gasped, "Angela...baby...don't! I want...if you touch me like that I'm going to lose control completely."

"Good," she whispered, and she touched him softly, then with confidence, making him groan her name on a ragged breath. Then he pushed her down into the soft grass.

She was waiting for him when he moved to join with her.

CHAPTER EIGHT

KENT was in the kitchen with Charlotte when Angela came down the next morning. He was laughing at something Charlotte had said. Angela stopped in the kitchen door, watching them.

Her lover. She had never had a lover before, only the man she had married so many years ago. Last night seemed an erotic dream, although she had never dreamed that kind of fulfillment in her wildest fantasies.

He was relaxed in his chair at the kitchen table, his back to her. He was, as always, wearing a tailored shirt that he could have worn to any business meeting, and immaculate pants. Angela wondered if he owned anything like jeans or sweatpants, tried to imagine having the nerve to try to buy him something like that.

She remembered how she had felt when she woke this morning. The unaccustomed awareness of her own body, the tingling sensitivity that was the aftermath of Kent's loving.

Loving. She had to try to control that kind of thinking. It was not going to be love. An affair, an exciting, passionate affair, and one day it would be over.

Charlotte finished telling the tale of her Mexican wedding to Harvey, the witness who had cried for them and flooded them with an incomprehensible barrage of Spanish well-wishing, the taxi driver who had refused to take his fare when he realized they were newlyweds. She shook back her short gray hair and saw Angela for the first time.

"Honey, come on in. Kent's made coffee—a vile brew, but a real eye-opener."

Angela went to the coffeepot. "You guys are early birds. It's only six-thirty!"

Charlotte laughed. She did that a lot these days. "Kent's the early bird—he always was. I remember when he was a kid, he'd be up at five and..."

Angela turned with her cup and found Kent's eyes on her. She flushed from what was in them. She had wondered if morning would come and he would be cool again, a stranger, but how could he ever be a stranger after what had happened last night?

"Hi," she said. She couldn't seem to make her voice any stronger.

"Good morning." His voice was husky too. "You look nice."

She was wearing a drifting caftan that Harvey had given her for Christmas last year. It must be the green color he liked, because the thing totally hid her shape.

Lord, she couldn't talk at all, could only remember last night under the moonlight. Afterward, Kent leaning over her, stroking her softly, whispering, "You look nice...beautiful...magic." Then he had kissed her again and she had felt that his arms were forever and he had said in a strange, husky voice, "I didn't mean to ravish you out in the bushes."

"Didn't you?" she had asked gently, feeling the soft confusion of his waving hair with her fingers, loving that shaken sound in his voice.

"I just wanted somewhere we would be alone. I was going to take my time." He had kissed her and she had come close into his arms, so that it had been a few moments before he could say, "Seduce you slowly... irresistibly."

She had laughed then, hearing her own husky amusement on the night air.

"Well..." His laughter had mingled with hers, then he had touched her, a soft intimate caress, and her amusement had turned to a gasp. He had buried his face in her hair, murmuring, "I like laughing with you, but I could have brought a blanket, at least."

Then she had confessed in a whisper that she had never done this before, out in the open with only the stars and the moon. "Nor me either," he had admitted. Then there had been no words, only warmth and heated touches, overwhelming passion and the breathless wonder of their loving.

It was in his eyes now. He was watching her as she came to the table. Charlotte was saying something and Angela realized that she was looking at her, waiting for some kind of answer. She flushed, and Kent smiled.

"What?" she asked Charlotte.

"I said what do you think? Scrambled or fried?"

Eggs, Angela realized. "It doesn't matter."

Kent said, "Will you come to Vancouver next weekend?"

Angela whispered, "Yes."

Charlotte was staring at her and she pushed her hand through her hair, feeling confused. Why had he asked her now? Why not later, when they were alone? Or last night?

Charlotte picked up her cup, said wryly, "I must have missed something here. Anybody want to tell me what's going on?"

Angela said, "No," breathlessly, while Kent said, "Angela's coming to Vancouver next weekend."

"I got that, but what are you going to——?" Charlotte stopped abruptly, said tightly, "Just be careful, will you? I don't want either of you hurt."

Angela tried to look away from Kent's eyes, but couldn't. Charlotte said, "I'll take coffee up to Harvey."

When she was gone, Angela shivered and stared into her coffee. "I don't want to be hurt either."

Kent said, "I wouldn't do anything to hurt you," which proved he did not really know the full effect he had on her. Then he said huskily, I want to kiss you good morning, but I'm not sure I'd be able to control what happened next."

She thought of last night, Kent groaning her name and taking her body with wild need. And that other time, in the living room of this house, when a fleeting touch, a kiss, had somehow burst into passion.

He picked up his cup, put it down again and said unsteadily, "I see you know what I mean."

She needed time to get her balance. She had to find the strength to do this thing right. He must never know that it was not just passion and liking. It was loving, the kind of need and desire that went forever. She wanted Vancouver next weekend, and she wanted the days between. Everything. His problems, his frowns...his babies. She had been crazy thinking it mattered where a man lived, how much money he had. Somehow she would manage, so long as...

The horrible thing was that she kept remembering his saying they could get married. Not love, he hadn't said a word about love. He'd made the offer after he had pressured her into telling him about Ben and the baby, and he'd felt somehow responsible for her pain then. Natural, because he was the man who looked after everyone else's problems. His mother in the big house. Charlotte, strewing problems around like a dog shaking water after a swim.

The moment had passed and the offer was gone. A good thing, because it would be disaster when she felt like this. She might be insane enough to agree, even though he didn't love her. Didn't she knew enough to learn from her one disastrous marriage?

Harvey came down in his bathrobe, carrying his coffee and holding Charlotte's hand. Charlotte looked quiet and happy.

In the end, Angela made breakfast while Kent set the table and Charlotte and Harvey discussed turning the two back bedrooms upstairs into a big sun room with a patio. Harvey thought they might as well, because why would they ever need five bedrooms. Angela thought she would move into the carriage house soon, because they should have the freedom of their own house.

Barney and Sally came with Jake and Wendy. Everyone ended up in the big kitchen, with coffee and the remnants of breakfast, Wendy fussing gently in Angela's arms and Jake asking Kent endless questions about Canada and the Mounties.

Sally made an exasperated sound and said to Kent, "He thinks the Mounties are the greatest thing ever since he saw that movie last week."

Kent did not seem to mind. He looked bemused and a bit overwhelmed by this noisy confusion, but he answered Jake's questions patiently while Barney and Harvey argued about Barney's design of a sailboat pulpit and Sally announced that Wendy was sleeping through her two o'clock feeding now.

The men eventually adjourned to the living room, leaving the women with the mess. "You notice, Jake went with them," Angela pointed out to Sally.

"Oh, yes. My son's turning into a real little chauvinist." Sally sounded proud rather than irritated, and Angela laughed.

All day she was aware of Kent, through the talking and the preparations for a late lunch, through taking Wendy upstairs to change her diaper and sitting on the living-room floor playing marbles with Jake. They hardly said a word to each other, but she noticed when he played a game of chess with Barney. Then, later, he went out to look at the old gas barbecue with Harvey. Jake went with him, holding his hand rather fiercely.

Charlotte was standing beside Angela as Jake and Kent walked through the patio doors together. She said oddly, "He's part of the family. Just like that. All these years I've felt as if he were a stranger."

Angela turned to her and saw unshed tears in Charlotte's eyes. If Kent wove his way into every part of Angela's life, what would there be for her when it was over?

He left in the late afternoon, saying goodbye to them all, then catching Angela's hand and demanding, "Come with me to my car."

It was not going to be a secret from her family, this affair with Kent. She went with him. Outside, on the veranda, he took her in his arms and with one kiss he turned the memories to flames. She wrapped her arms around his shoulders, his neck, her fingers through his hair, holding him closer.

When he released her, they were both trembling.

"That's how I'll dream of you," he said. "Looking like this."

She stared up at him, wanting to pull him back into her arms, but seeing his eyes changing from heat to something that was almost ice. His mouth hardened into a straight line and he said, "I'll pick you up on Friday at six," and she wondered what made him look so grim as he turned away from her.

There was an uncomfortable silence in the house when she went back. She knew what they were thinking: Angela going away for a weekend with a man. She had never done that before.

Jake was the only one who said anything that day. He was on the floor with a book of pictures open in front of him. He looked up when the others fell silent. "I guess you got over not liking Kent, didn't you, Aunt Angie? Can I come with you to see the Mounties?''

On Tuesday Barney told her she was crazy.

"What do you think he wants of you?" he demanded angrily, pacing back and forth in front of her cutting table. "Where do you think it can lead?"

Nowhere.

Barney banged the cutting table with his fist. "Angie, have some sense! He's a money man. He's rich, for crying out loud, and he lives in a different world from yours! The only place it's going to go is straight into his bed!"

Angela swallowed and stared at the window material on her table. Had she cut that window out backward? She tried to figure it out, but her mind got lost in mentally turning the piece over, matching it to the fabric.

"Angie!"

"Don't shout at me, Barney." She dropped her scissors and met his eyes. "It's too late. We're having an affair and . . . and that's the way it is."

He thumped the table again. "Are you crazy?"

"Barney, I don't need big brother protection." She could feel the sick knowledge inside that Barney's warning was probably every bit as valid as back when he'd tried to keep her away from Ben.

"You need something! He's going to hurt you, Angie!"

Of course he was right. She shrugged. "I thought you liked him."

"He's going to eat you alive. What do you think you're going to get out of this? He might offer to keep you in an apartment somewhere, but you can be bloody sure he's not taking you to meet his mother!"

"His grandmother," she corrected automatically. "Charlotte's his mother. And Charlotte married your dad.'' If she had grabbed when Kent had suggested they could get married, she would have met his grandmother, seen the big house he grew up in. But she would always know he was trapped. It would not work without loving.

Barney said, ''Charlotte's a misfit anyway, a fifty-one-year-old who hasn't ever quite grown up. Do you think he's going to marry you? A canvas worker?''

She grabbed the scissors to stop her hands trembling. ''Barney, please stop!'' She gritted her teeth and said rigidly, ''It was too late the first time I saw him. So don't make it any harder for me—please!''

A customer came in at that moment, carrying a black, oily hunk of metal, frowning and muttering, ''Can you get this slug out for me? Without disturbing the other one?''

Barney and the customer went into the back to wrestle with the problem and Angela cut out a new windshield for the dodger she was making, this time getting it the right way around. Her pile of scraps was getting monstrous, and she was only two days into the week. She'd be making sheet bags for weeks out of the remnants if she didn't smarten up and get her mind on her job.

On Wednesday a shop in Bellingham called and asked if she had a catalog for her Sailing Rags. She said she was putting one together, and the buyer asked for an assortment of the clothes.

''A variety of sizes, colors,'' the woman said. ''Let's say two dozen pieces. Do you have pants that match those shirts? Good. And put us down for a copy of that catalog when it's ready. Two copies, and I'll send one on to our store in Portland.''

Angela packed on Thursday night. She would take her bag to work with her on Friday. Six, Kent had said, and she needed every minute until then to work on cutting out the garments for the new order. After packing she went over to Barney's, because Sally had asked her to come, but what Sally really wanted was to be sure that Angela had herself on some kind of birth control.

Harvey did not say anything, but Angela did not think he was happy about her weekend away. He was more of a father to her than the man who lived in England. It hurt her that he was worried, that she was the cause. She did not know what to say to him and found herself avoiding being alone with him.

On Friday, Charlotte drove to the shop in the middle of the morning and asked Angela to come to lunch with her. Angela was in the middle of the last series of cuttings.

"I can't, Charlotte. I've got to get this done. I want to have at least the small shirts done today. I promised that order would go out next Thursday."

Charlotte circled the cutting table uneasily. "Can I help?"

Angela had an idea that Charlotte at a sewing-machine would be a disaster. Her new mother-in-law tended to do most things with more energy than care.

"No, I've got to do it myself." She cut the last pair of large pants, stuck a label on the bundle with a piece of masking tape. Pants. Large. Women's. "What about Monday?" she suggested to Charlotte.

"Monday?"

"Lunch. You wanted to go to lunch." She was the one who was going nuts, simultaneously dreading and yearning for six o'clock. "We could go to lunch on Monday."

Charlotte picked up a scrap of material, folded it in half, then folded it again. "Angie, this thing with Kent..."

If one more person told her she was making a mistake, she was going to start screaming and throwing things. She looked at Charlotte, knew that she could not scream at her. You could scream at Barney, but Charlotte was somehow too fragile.

Charlotte said, "Angela, don't...don't play with him, will you?"

She gasped, "What?"

"I mean, he's not a Charles or a Saul. You go out with them and all along you know it's not going anywhere. If they get too close you shut them off." Charlotte was talking quickly, avoiding Angela's eyes. "You won't do that with Kent, will you? He's—— You see, he isn't a person who's ever been able to take things lightly."

Charlotte was afraid she would hurt Kent. Charlotte, who had been telling her only a week ago that Kent was cold. It would have been funny, except Angela felt more like crying.

He came at five minutes to six, driving his Chrysler. Everyone was there, Barney and Harvey and Jake. Even Sally had just happened to stop by, on her way back from the supermarket with Wendy.

Kent shook hands with Harvey, nodded to Barney, who frowned back at him. He kissed Charlotte on the cheek and said hello to Sally as he touched the baby's head lightly. He ended up standing beside Angela's machine. She pulled out the pair of pants she was sewing and snapped the thread.

"Are you ready?" Not hello, or something about how nice she looked, just that gruff question.

She nodded, switched the machine off and folded the half-finished pants on top of a stack of cut-out clothing. Her overnight bag was under the counter that held the coffee. She got it and he took it out of her hand. Everyone was standing there, watching, and she didn't know what to say to them all. One way or another, they all disapproved, except Jake.

She went to her nephew and promised, "I'll bring you back a postcard of a Mountie."

Kent was behind her, not touching her. She wished he would take her arm or her hand, or even smile. It would give her the courage to think of something to say to them all.

Sally said, "Enjoy yourself," then flushed a deep red when she realized the implications of telling Angela to have fun on a weekend away with a man.

Angela said abruptly, "I'll see you all Sunday night." Kent was holding the door and she went out quickly.

He was not looking particularly happy either. Maybe he had decided this was a bad idea, too, although she would have thought he could have called with some excuse—a sudden business meeting or an attack of appendicitis.

Inside his car, she did not know where to look. She could feel him beside her, could see him out of the corner of her eye when she stared out of the window. He drove silently to the intersection then turned and headed the Chrysler toward the ferry terminal.

She said brightly, "You brought your car. I thought you might have come in the jet."

He shifted lanes and turned off into the ferry terminal. There were three cars ahead of him at the toll booth. He said grimly, "The Lear is having its hundred-hour maintenance." After a minute of uncomfortable silence, he added, "It should be out of the hangar tomorrow. You can go back that way on Sunday if you want."

Sunday. Forty-eight hours. She stared at her hands lying inert on her pants. She had wanted to go shopping this week, to find something elegant and irresistible to wear for him. There had been no time, though. So she had raided her closet last night for the best outfit she could find to wear to work. She couldn't wear a skirt, not when she would be crawling all over cutting tables. So she had worn rust-colored pants that were cut elegantly enough for a dinner out, and a matching jacket over a peach-colored silk blouse.

Maybe he would have preferred her in a skirt. Or perhaps, after a week to think it over, he was wondering why he had been insane enough to invite her for a whole weekend.

Forty-eight hours, and they already had nothing to say. She picked up the road map on the seat between them and stared at the colored lines, forcing herself to figure out the maze of border crossings and wonder if he would go north on 15. As if it mattered which highway he took.

When their turn came at the toll booth, Kent had his wallet out and ready. Angela watched him putting the change back in, the green American notes along with the brightly colored Canadian money. They didn't even live in the same country. Different money. Different political systems. Different lives. He made money and she made clothes and canvas work for boats. He wore a three-piece suit to work and she didn't even own an evening gown, hadn't been to a social event where she would need one since the summer she was sixteen when her parents had taken her with them to San Francisco.

He pulled into the lane the toll attendant had directed him to. The ferry was not there. She supposed it would be about half an hour before the next one came. Thirty minutes in silence, in a car with a stranger. That was almost as long as forever.

He turned toward her, his eyes somber and his lips in that thin line. "I take it no one back there approves of your going away with me this weekend?"

She shrugged and pleated the crease of her pants with her thumb and forefinger. "Barney thinks you're up to no good with me, and Harvey's worried. But Charlotte thinks I'm the one who's up to no good with you." Her voice sounded as nervous as she felt. Twenty-nine years old, and she didn't know how to make small talk in a situation like this. An affair, and she had no idea how to handle any of it.

"What about you?" He was looking for the answer in her face. "Do you want to back out?"

She swallowed. "Do you?"

A muscle jumped in his jaw. "I'm here, aren't I?"

She dropped her eyes from his. "So am I."

"Despite the opposition?" She nodded. "I'm glad," he said softly. She looked and found his eyes had lost the coolness.

"It must have been awkward for you back there."

"Hmm. They were all surrounding you like a protective army." He touched her nose, stroked his finger along the short slope. "I thought I might have to fight for you."

"Barney might have been willing," she said wryly. "He's always been willing to come to blows for me."

"He probably broke their noses," murmured Kent. "I thought about that too. If he was willing to get a broken nose to protect you from his own brother, I figured I could be in for trouble."

She laughed, but knew that he was not about to come to blows for her. A minute ago she could have told him she had second thoughts and he would have driven her back to the family who wanted to protect her.

She knew it was all supposed to be a joke when he said, "I figured that with Barney's muscles, I'd probably come out of the battle the worse. It's just as well it didn't come to fighting to get you away, because you might not find me so attractive with a broken nose."

"You'd get blood all over your car."

He laughed. He took something wrapped in tissue out of his breast pocket and unwrapped it. "I was going to give these to you later, in suitably romantic surroundings, but——"

She stared at the tiny scraps of gold lying in tissue in his hand. Earrings. He had said he wanted to see bits of gold dangling against her throat.

She touched the tiny golden sea gulls. "They're beautiful."

He cleared his throat. "Will you wear them?"

"Yes." It was only a whisper. Could she ever say no to him, about anything? She fumbled with the fasteners for the hoops in her ears to take them off. "Will you put them in for me?" she asked, afraid that her own hands would be shaking too much.

He swallowed, and she had the strangest feeling that he was afraid. Of what? He put the tissue down on the seat between them, picked up one of the tiny charms hanging from a golden stud, and said, "I've never done this before. I don't want to hurt you."

I love you. She almost said it. Her lips were parted and she could feel tears behind her eyes. "Just...just put the post through the little hole in my ear," she whispered. "It won't hurt if you're gentle with it."

He did it very slowly, very carefully. Then he slid the tiny backing piece on to the post, and she did not move when he pushed it a little too tight, not wanting to tell him that he had hurt her. She remembered what she had thought the first time she saw him, that he was unfeeling about Charlotte, unsympathetic. But he was touching her so gently, his face intent and his fingers almost trembling against her neck and her ear.

"There," he said when the second earring was secure.

She watched his eyes on her and said, "Do you like them on me?"

He touched her neck with his lips, a soft caress to the white flesh where the little golden bird brushed as she moved her head. "You make them quite beautiful, Angela."

She whispered, "Thank you," thinking she would probably wear them forever.

"How about an ice cream?"

She had put her hand on the side of his neck, had turned her face as he moved his lips from her neck. She wanted him to kiss her on the lips, needed his touch on her. She said softly, "We're waiting for the ferry."

"Yeah." He swallowed and her fingers moved to the place where his Adam's apple had jerked. "It won't be here for twenty minutes or so, and..."

She leaned forward to kiss him and he jerked back.

"Lady, if you don't want your reputation in this town totally destroyed, you'd better get out of this car!"

Her lips parted.

He said, "If you kiss me, I'm not going to be responsible for what happens next."

She felt excitement crawling through her chest. Her fingers came to rest on his lips. "In broad daylight in the ferry lineup?"

He covered her fingers with his hand and pulled them away from his face. "If you're counting on my inhibitions to keep you safe, you're on pretty dangerous ground." He did not smile at all.

Barney was wrong, she thought with a dizzy certainty. It was more than an affair. She wasn't the only one who was stumbling around in the clouds.

They left the car parked in the ferry lineup and went for ice-cream cones. Outside the confines of the car they managed to talk more easily. She told him about the new order for Sailing Rags. He told her about the waterfront property he had bid on this last week, still upset with himself for losing out to an opposing buyer.

"If I'd bid ten thousand dollars more," he said, licking a dribble of chocolate ice cream that was trickling down the side of his cone. He shrugged. "It was a sealed bid, and I guessed it wrong."

She licked her cone and asked, "Can't you try to buy it off the fellow who did get the bid?"

He shook his head. "I could, if I wanted it that badly. I wanted that property, but not at that price. It wasn't worth that much to me."

She wondered how much she was worth to him, and knew that she must never ask.

The ferry came and Kent drove them onto the car deck. He caught her hand as they were going up the stairs to the upper deck on the ferry, and she was finally able to throw caution to the winds. As she had told Barney, it was far too late for her to start trying to keep safe now.

They went out on deck on the ferry, the wind in their faces and the sea gulls flying along behind the boat. Kent bent to kiss the place where the tiny golden sea gulls brushed her neck, and she shivered and whispered, "That old woman beside the rails—she's staring at us."

He took both her hands in his. "I don't think it's going to make any difference who disapproves of us, Angela. Your relatives or my relatives, total strangers. I'm taking you home with me."

Home. It sounded like a place that was theirs, for being together. Forever, she thought, and she knew she was losing even that control, the ability to know her dreams were only fantasy.

"Will I meet your mother?" she asked, staring out at the gulls flying, twisting and gliding on the wind currents, hoping for handouts.

He linked his fingers with hers. "Let's not add complications to what could be a perfect weekend."

Could be. Two days with him.

His apartment was bright and simply decorated, with big windows looking out over Sunset Beach. It was dark when he let her into it. They had stopped for dinner at a quiet restaurant somewhere between the border and the inner city of Vancouver. She didn't know where it had been, just that there were soft lights and music, and she could not even remember what it was she had eaten.

Inside his apartment, she moved to the window, staring out at the skyline, lights streaking over the water.

"English Bay," he said, coming up behind her. "And that's Sunset Beach. This area used to be all big old houses, but in the last thirty years the apartment buildings have slowly eaten up the old family houses."

He put his arms around her and she leaned against him, feeling the solidness of his broad chest, his breath tickling her ear. She had taken her jacket off as she crossed the big living room with its thick carpet. Now he took it out of her hand, tossed it over a nearby sofa and pulled her back into his arms, his fingers sliding along the silk covering on her arms.

"I want you," he murmured, bending to touch her neck with his lips, spreading his hands across her midriff, then sliding up to the curve of her breasts. "Do you know I've been aching for you all week? Do you know how much——?"

He broke off and she turned in his arms. She wanted to say she was his, that she would stay forever if he asked her. That she loved him. She could not say anything, just stared at him with her eyes wide and her heart thundering in her ears.

CHAPTER NINE

ANGELA woke in Kent's arms. The first thing she saw was his face, his eyes deep and blue, watching her. Then, when his lips covered hers, her eyes lost their focus and the wonderful dizziness surged up over her.

She had a vague memory of waking in the night, of Kent lifting her from the soft carpet where they had made love, carrying her through the dark rooms and laying her on a big bed. Then dreamy, slow loving that surged from tenderness to breathlessness.

"What do you want to do today?" he asked now, his voice buried against her throat.

She twisted in his arms and said, "Um..."

He laughed against her throat. "After last night, I don't think I'm capable!" But when he lifted his head his blue eyes turned almost black and he said raggedly, "I could be wrong, though. Let's find out."

Later, she made him breakfast from the meager pickings in his kitchen while he made the coffee.

"You should buy groceries," she told him. "With a kitchen like this, you don't need to eat out."

"Takeout," he said, watching her as she moved about his kitchen. She had forgotten to bring a dressing gown and was wearing one of his shirts. It fell to mid-thigh, but when she moved he was very aware of what was under it. Nothing. He swallowed and told himself he could not spend the whole weekend grabbing her and pulling her back into his bed. "Takeout," he repeated, determined to have *some* control over himself.

"McDonald's and Kentucky Fried, but I bring it back here to eat."

She turned from the stove, a frying-pan flipper in one hand and a pot holder in the other. "You told me you cooked your own meals here."

He grinned. "Occasionally. Frozen dinners mostly," he admitted.

She scowled. "And fast food the rest of the time?" He nodded. "You mean you eat that junk all the time? You can't do that. All that fried food, and not enough vegetables."

He could not remember anyone caring what he ate before, and he wondered what he was going to do when she decided that it was over. He hated the thought of joining the others she had discarded, Charles and Saul and heaven knew what other names.

But she had not given herself to any of them. And she did not give herself lightly. So maybe there was a chance for them.

"We could go grocery shopping," he offered.

"You can't eat properly for just two days."

He wondered what she would say if he asked her to stay, and thought he had better watch it or he would be out in the cold with Charles. Hadn't she made it completely clear that she did not want a serious relationship?

He insisted on doing the dishes, and she said she wanted to see Stanley Park. She even had the nerve to add, "But you can't go in a suit. Don't you have any jeans?" He shook his head, smiling, and she said, "Then we should go and get you some."

They went to a menswear shop where he often shopped, and he laughed when she told him they could buy the jeans for half the price in a department store. Then she chose an expensive knit shirt that was soft and red, with an open collar she liked because she could just see the beginning of the fair hairs that curled on his chest.

She wanted to buy the shirt for him.

"No," he said flatly, telling the owner, "Put all this on my account."

The man nodded and went off to write up the account, giving Angela a look that showed he wondered who she was and how long she would last. Not long, she thought, but if she didn't get outside and get some air she might start an argument with Kent right here in this sedate shop.

Outside, she took slow, deep breaths of air, trying to tell herself it didn't matter. But why would he not accept a gift from her? It made her think of Barney saying she would end up living in an apartment Kent had paid for, his kept woman. That scared her silly, because if he asked for that, she might be foolish enough to say yes, and it was never going to be enough. She would be back to the same thing again, wanting love to grow into a family, trying to hold on to nothing.

He had suggested marriage once, but he'd been feeling sorry for her. He was never going to ask again. He wanted her. Passion, yes, but how long would that last if he did not love her?

The car was locked. She stood beside it, waiting, wondering if she should not heed the nervous voice that told her it was time to leave, find a bus and get back where she belonged before he sent her away.

He was wearing the red shirt as he came along the pavement to the car. And a frown. "Why did you run off like that?"

"If you can buy me gold earrings, why can't I buy you that shirt?" Her voice cracked and that made her angry. "What is it? My body, and your gifts?"

He stared down at her, that muscle jumping in his jaw. "Damn it, Angela, I'm not having you buy my clothes! I can afford it a hell of a lot easier than you can."

She lifted her chin and stared at him. He was carrying a bag that must hold his other clothes. "How much was it?" She heard her own voice and wondered wildly what she was trying to do. But she could not seem to stop the words. "Do you think you can buy me too, Kent?"

His eyes went cold and hard. "Are you for sale?"

Oh, God. She turned away, stumbling on the curb. Where the hell was there to go? A strange city, a strange country. And the only things were his white, expensive car, and his hand catching at her arm to stop her falling.

"Let go of me!" She spat the words as if he were her deadly enemy. He released her abruptly.

He opened the door for her, then went around to the driver's side and started the car. He did not say a word to her, and she wondered how all the tenderness could suddenly have exploded into anger. She stared at her hands and they weren't shaking, not visibly, but she was shivering inside like a coil wound too tight.

She would not have been surprised if he had taken her all the way back to Port Townsend without saying a word, or out to the airport and into that Lear jet and good riddance. She was pretty sure she had messed everything up with that stupid argument and that accusation about trying to buy her. Of all the damned stupid things to say! "Are you for sale?" he had asked, and she had felt as if he slapped her, hard. She blinked several times and kept the tears from spilling over.

It seemed to take forever, moving through the traffic, stopping more than starting. She stared at a bus in front of them for a long time, then a red sports car driven by a young girl with long blond hair.

Then, abruptly, the city gave way to a winding drive and they were speeding through tall trees. He stopped, finally, parking in a smallish parking lot, between a grassy slope and a sea wall. When he turned off the engine, the silence was almost oppressive.

He got out of the car.

In front of the car, there were people on the sea wall—a woman pushing a baby in a carriage, two boys on roller skates. Kent walked away from the car as if Angela were not even there, crossing the walk and staring out over the water. She would hardly blame him if he was wondering how quickly he could get rid of her.

He had not shut his door, a crazy detail that was not like him at all. She got out of the car, closed her door and then went around to close his door too. She was in no hurry to get to him, had no idea what she could say to cancel out being a hot-tempered idiot.

He must have heard her coming, even over the grass. She stopped just before the cement walk of the sea wall. He turned away from the water and watched her come. Two men in shorts jogged past between them.

"I lost my temper," he said finally. "I didn't mean what I said."

She shook her head. It had hurt, but of course he had not meant it. "It was...a stupid argument."

He wanted to touch her, to somehow erase that hurt look in her eyes. She had tried to give him something, but he had slapped it away. What the hell could he do to change that now? Ask her for the money to pay for the shirt she had wanted to give? "I was wrong about the shirt." He shrugged uncomfortably, then offered, "Next time..."

She looked away from him. "Why didn't you want me to give——?"

"I don't know." But he did know. Easy enough to buy things for her; harder to accept a gift. No one had ever given him a spontaneous present before. Only the obligatory offerings under the designer Christmas tree in the cold old house. He pressed his lips together, felt his hands clench into fists at his side and admitted, "I don't have much practice with relationships."

Her eyes jerked back to his, wide and green and un-comfortable. He felt a sick premonition. She would leave him. Although he could touch her body and stir her passion, sharing breathless excitement, it would never be enough to hold her. Relationship, he had said, but she was the woman who had been avoiding relationships ever since that bastard had walked out on her.

"Is this a relationship?" she whispered.

Oh, God! His heart was beating with impossible dreams; while just the word "relationship" was enough to panic her. She was staring at his face, must know his thoughts. She could always see right through him, the only person who ever had. His jaw jutted out and he muttered grimly, "It's what we make of it, isn't it?"

They stood four feet apart, uncomfortable. He heard his own stilted voice. "Do you still want to see the park?"

"Yes, please."

Keep it light. Don't put pressure on her. He knew how it would end. Not happy ever after, together, but himself sitting in a cold office staring out over the city. Alone, as he had always been; but so much more empty after having a taste of loving.

He could not hold her gaze, but had to look away, stare at the duck walking along the grass between the parking lot and the sea wall.

Angela knew that she had better smarten up, stop cre-ating awkward situations, or Kent would be running to get away from her. She gave herself a silent lecture as he locked the car.

Then they were walking up the hill under the trees, not touching.

"Have you done this before?" How could she have asked that? Of all the stupid, foolish questions! Of course he had. She was not the first and she would not be the last.

"You mean Stanley Park?" He turned to her, half smiling, his face relaxed until he saw the tension in her. Then the lines in his face deepened and he said quietly, "If you mean women in my apartment, then yes, I have."

Why had she asked?

He said rather grimly, "But I've never..." then swallowed what had to be anger and changed whatever he had been about to say. "But I've never done this. Wandering around Stanley Park."

She bit her lip. "Does that mean I'm different?" She squeezed her eyes closed. "Don't—please don't answer that! I—— How can you not have wandered around here? If I lived here——" Lord, that was even worse. Next she would be asking if she could move in with him. She gulped and amended it to, "If I worked in those skyscrapers—if I worked there, I'd be over here for lunch every day."

He caught her hands and pulled her around to face him. "Angela, stop it!"

She stared at his chin, pulled in an unsteady breath and muttered, "I'm no good at this," and saw his mouth and chin looking grimmer than ever. How the hell could she take it lightly? It did not feel light at all. When she looked at him, her heart stopped and she knew she would never be able to let another man touch her, because Kent would be in her dreams forever.

He turned her hands in his and stared down at her palms. "I'm not sharing this weekend with some other woman. I'm spending it with you. Because I want to." He looked up then, released her hand and tilted her chin up to make her eyes meet his. "And I would hope that you're here because you want to be with me."

She nodded numbly.

"Isn't that enough, then?"

"Yes, of course." She had never before lied to people she cared about, but he was turning everything upside-down and the truth would have been impossible.

He frowned. She stepped back from him, stared past him up the hill. A path joining another path. A young boy with his dog. What would he say if she told him she loved him? What if she told him she wanted to live with him, to share with him...forever? He would think she was insane, because she was pretty sure that only last week she had told him the last thing she wanted was to get serious about him.

He held his hand out and she took it. They started up the path. He said casually, "Usually I have business lunches. And business weekends, for that matter. So you'll have to show me how to behave in a park."

His leg brushed hers as they climbed the hill. She managed to make her own voice light. "Now that you're in the right costume, you'll find it's easy to waste away a Saturday."

Through the monkeys and the bears in the zoo she kept control of that suicidal part of her that wanted to tell him she loved him. Whatever the rules were when you were having an affair, she knew that asking about the other women in his life had to be breaking them all, but saying "I love you" might be worse.

After the bears, they went into the aquarium to watch the whales. Then lunch at the Pavilion and a long lazy walk along the sea wall. Then back to his apartment, and she could not look at him through all the drive back.

It was never going to work. In a few moments, when the door to his apartment closed on them, she thought he would touch her and everything else would cease to matter. But morning would come, and tomorrow he would send her off on his jet and it would be as if she had never been here.

Would he ask her to come back next weekend? How many weekends? And if she could somehow say no, would he come after her again, claiming her as his... mistress?

Would he ever ask her to be his wife again? It wouldn't work, couldn't work. She could never fit into his life here in Vancouver, any more than he could exist in sleepy Port Townsend. But she wished she could try, because nothing less would do either.

The telephone was ringing as Kent unlocked the door into his apartment. She walked past him, past the ringing telephone that he was reaching for, to the window and the water outside. She stared at the sailboats, weekend sailors dotting English Bay with white triangles and colorful spinnakers.

She wondered about the house where he spent the other part of his life. Where it was. What it looked like. Whether he would take her there if she asked. She wondered how many women there had been in this apartment with him, staying for a night or a weekend, and whether any of them had been taken to the house he had grown up in.

Behind her, his voice was patient. "Yes...I don't think you have to worry about that... No, Mother, you can't do anything about it if he wants to paint his house blue. You can't see it anyway, unless you go up to that dormer room on the third floor."

His mother. No, that wasn't right. His grandmother, except that his grandparents had adopted him, so that must make them his parents really.

"No, not today. I'll call you early in the week."

She turned. He was standing with one hand on the antique rolltop desk in the alcove of the living room, his eyes watching Angela as he talked. She should turn away, not stand here so obviously listening, but her gaze was caught in his and she just stood like a fool, staring at him, feeling her pulse thudding through her body and not knowing if it was fear or anger or excitement.

"Sorry, but it's impossible. No... no, it's business."

What was business? She tried to swallow the dryness in her throat, but all she managed was a spasm. She heard him say goodbye and knew Barney was right. She was going to be sealed off, trapped in a segment of his life that didn't touch the rest.

He was crossing the room to her. He was going to take her in his arms, and even that was not going to work. She turned away nervously. "You can go if you want. She wants you to come over there, doesn't she? I don't mind if you——"

"I mind." He took her shoulders and slowly turned her to face him. "She can wait."

"When I'm gone?" He had said business. As if he were hiding her. "Does she know about me?"

"No." He brushed her lips with his. "Do we have to talk about her now? I'd much rather make love with you."

He took her wrists and lifted her hands up to rest against his chest. Through the soft knit shirt she could feel the hard curve of his male breasts.

"Kent, I don't..."

He bent to kiss her cheek, the side of her throat. Her fingers curled into his chest. She had not realized that her eyes had closed until he kissed her lids tenderly. Then he left her and she was standing alone.

He did something to the stereo built into a bookcase and music came, soft and provocative. He moved to the window and the heavy curtains slid across to make darkness inside. She stood, knowing he would come to her, waiting in the darkness.

His feet hardly made a sound on the thick carpet. She heard a faint click and Kent's silhouette straightened from the dimly glowing light he had turned on.

"Dance with me, Angela."

She went into his arms. He held her intimately against him, moving slowly to the music. She buried her face in his shoulder and felt the touch of his lips on her neck, his hands holding her close so that she felt his hard masculinity burning against her.

How could she want him when she felt frozen inside, knowing there was no real place for her in his life?

"Angela...want me, darling." His lips sought her face, covering her lips and her cheeks, her eyelids and her forehead with soft, heated kisses. "Feel what you do to me." His voice was hoarse against her flesh. "For God's sake, baby, don't shut me out!"

She whimpered and he took her open mouth with his. His hands slid to her hips, her buttocks, and he felt her body tremble against his. "Yes," he said against her throbbing lips. "Yes, darling."

He took her down with him. She felt the soft carpet under her head, saw the dark shape of the man she loved blanking out the faint glow of light as he leaned over her. He covered her breasts with his hands and she felt his hands stop, motionless, holding her, warmth through the sweater she had worn against the September chill.

"Please," she whispered, knowing that touching was not enough, would never be enough. His hands moved and his body came down against hers. Gently, slowly, he took the sweater away, then the lacy thing that was underneath.

Then there was nothing but their naked, heated flesh. When he tried to move slowly, to drive her to that frantic edge of loving before he lost control himself, she touched him and caressed his flesh with her mouth and her hands.

He groaned her name and moved over her, joined with her, hard and needing and thrusting into the heart of her. She heard her voice and it sounded like another woman's need, whispering words of love, begging.

"Please...Kent...love me...oh...please...I love you..."

She woke in darkness, in his arms. She lay very still, hardly breathing, feeling his shoulder pillowing her head, his other arm heavy across her midriff.

She stared at nothing, darkness with shapes in it. Then she closed her eyes and it was still darkness. Kent shifted in his sleep, murmuring something inaudible, his face pressing against her shoulder. His hand found her breast and he gave a murmur of contentment.

It had been afternoon, Kent's arms and his touch, his voice saying he wanted her, asking her to want him.

Want?

Had she really said those things? She squeezed her eyes tight and knew that she had. It was real, not some dream to wake from hot and frantic. She had told him she loved him. Begged him...oh, no! She couldn't have done that, could she? Her heart thudded against his arm. His lips moved against her shoulder and his hand caressed her, even in his sleep. She could feel her own reaction, could not seem to stop it even now with the memory of her own voice in the night.

"Please, Kent... Oh! Love me... I need you to love me...not just making love, but...darling, please!"

He had driven her so far beyond control that she had heard the echo of her own voice at the end, screaming. She felt a spasm at the pit of her stomach and knew it was no dream. Keep it light. That was hilarious, because she had lost it all, had not kept even a trace of control over her words or her body or her mind.

He had not said anything. He had held her in his arms and later he must have carried her here to his bed, because she could not remember walking. She had fallen asleep in his arms, and there had not been one word he could whisper to her then.

I love you. Those were the words he had not been able to say, the only words to answer a woman who had just laid herself bare in a man's arms. He hadn't said them.

She had to get out of here before he woke up, before his eyes opened. She could not bear to look into his blue gaze and see the discomfort that he would be feeling.

He moved when she shifted away. She stood beside his bed, naked, staring down at the shadow of his body tangled in the covers. He muttered something she could not quite hear, turned onto his stomach and flung his arm across the place where she had been.

She closed her eyes tightly, but she would have this picture in her heart forever. If she turned the light on, she knew the look that would be on his sleeping face. He would be vulnerable with sleep, younger without the tension lines.

She hugged herself and forced her legs to move, to turn and pick up her case from the corner near his wardrobe. She went with it into the bathroom and shut the door before she turned the light on.

She left the apartment without finding everything she had brought. Her things were scattered through his rooms, as if she were trying to claim a place there. She collected the makeup bag from the bathroom, the coat from the closet in the entrance hall, the clothes from the living-room carpet, strewn about carelessly, tangled with his.

There was a dress hanging in his wardrobe. She had brought it in case he wanted to go somewhere for dinner and dancing, or to the theater. She did not care if she ever saw the dress again. Or that fateful blouse with the long lace that tied it. That was in his wardrobe too, and she hoped she never saw it again. Her watch—she didn't know where that was, although she remembered Kent kissing her arm, her wrist, taking the watch off when his lips encountered it.

The corridor outside his apartment was empty and silent. She pushed in the button that locked his door and closed it behind her. Burning bridges, she thought, because now she could hardly pound on that door and wake him, asking to be let back in. He had not given her a key. Of course not, as she was only a weekend guest, but not having a key was symbolic of her real place in his life.

The elevator came at once. Kent's apartment was on the ninth floor, and she stepped into the little cage, staring at the door as it closed her in. Then she realized that she had forgotten to punch the button for the ground floor. She jabbed it so hard that her finger hurt and the elevator dropped with a fast hum that left her feeling slightly sick when the doors opened.

She stepped around a man with a tidy beard and a blond woman in his arms. They giggled and released each other, going into the elevator. Lovers, she thought dully, then she saw the wedding ring on the woman's finger, the matching ring on his.

Did she have to be so stupid? Barney had warned her, hadn't he? Just as he had tried to warn her about Ben. Next time she would go to Barney first and get his approval before she even went out to dinner with a man.

There was never going to be a next time. Never going to be another man.

The street was almost empty, lit from above, and the sky black overhead. The door to the apartment building swung shut silently behind her. She turned around and stared at it, stared at the panel of buttons. Locked out. She did not have a key. Of course she did not have a key. And she certainly was not going to buzz Kent in the middle of the night. What would she say? "I got out of your bed and ran out here because I couldn't face your knowing how desperately I love you, and now..."

She had no idea what time it was. A man walked along the pavement, his steps slowing as he neared Kent's building. She turned and studied the list of names and the little buttons. K. Ferguson. The footsteps stopped. Lord, it would be pretty awful if she had to buzz Kent to come down and chase off a strange man in the middle of the night!

The footsteps moved on.

She slung the bag over her shoulder and hurried along the empty pavement in the other direction. She could not see a pay telephone anywhere. If she hadn't been in such a desperate rush to get out of that apartment, she would have had the sense to call for a taxi. What was she going to do, walk the streets carrying an overnight bag?

A car drove past, slowly, and she felt abruptly conscious of herself as a woman alone on the street, carrying a bag as a glaring message that she was alone, did not live in the next building.

The lights were brighter ahead. She hurried, her shoes making the only noise around as she moved. When she saw the lights of a car turning on to the street ahead of her, she bent her head and walked more quickly, hoping she looked as if she were going somewhere in particular.

The car stopped. All around her, the buildings were tall, most of the windows dark. The apartment building beside her was another of those security things. No one could get in without a key. You had to buzz someone inside and . . .

"Hey, honey! Want a ride?"

She turned abruptly and ran up the stairs of the locked building.

"Hey, come on . . . come on for a ride, honey. We'll give you a good time."

She shoved her hand into the outside pocket of her bag. Heaven knew why she had brought her own keys for a weekend in Vancouver, but she pulled them out now and tried to look as if one of them would fit that door. Behind her she could hear two voices from the car, a muttered argument. One of them said something about going up to Davie Street and the engine roared.

This was not Port Townsend, a little town with sleepy habits and places she knew. Vancouver might be a quiet city compared to a place like New York, but obviously a woman was crazy to go wandering around the streets alone in the middle of the night.

She hurried toward the brighter lights ahead. Then, abruptly, she was out of the residential district of high-rise beach-front apartments.

A bus stop. She half ran along the pavement that was suddenly wide and no longer empty. A man walked by, staggering slightly, and she looked away. No buses coming. What time was it? Night, but there were cars driving past now and then. This was a wide street, probably full of cars in the daytime, but late on a Saturday night it was spooky, frightening.

A noisy group of people came out of the building behind her, three men and two women. One of the men smiled as he saw her and she turned away abruptly.

How many times did a bus come to this stop. Had the buses stopped running? Maybe they stopped at eleven, or at midnight. What time was it now?

She felt her back tensing, the skin crawling with nervousness every time someone came out of the building behind her. A pub. Why had they put the bus stop in front of a pub? What about women who came to catch a bus, alone in the middle of the night?

She did not have any Canadian money on her. Charlotte had told her not to bother going to the bank, just to take American and she could easily change it in any shop north of the border.

But what if the bus would not accept American money?

What if the bus never came?

She tried to look as if she knew what she was doing, waiting for a bus that was never going to come.

Sooner or later Kent would wake up. What would he do when he found her gone? She closed her eyes and realized how stupid she had been, running off in the middle of the night. It might be easier for him if he didn't have to face her after her lying in his arms begging him to love her, but he wasn't going to roll over and go back to sleep if he thought she was out alone on the city streets. Not Kent.

She hadn't left a note or anything.

"Ma'am? Are you all right?"

She jerked her eyes open—a police car, pulled up at the bus stop with the passenger window open and a young, stern face looking up at her.

She licked her dry lips. "I'm just waiting for a bus."

The young, official face frowned. "This isn't a very good neighborhood this time of night."

He didn't have to tell *her* that, she thought hysterically. "I—er—do you know when the next bus comes by?"

"I think you'd better get in for a moment, miss."

He pushed the door open and she wondered wildly if he was going to arrest her for...for what? Vagrancy? Wasn't it vagrancy if you had nowhere to go and no place to stay?

"Get in, miss."

She got into the car, pulled the door shut and thought of this young police officer escorting her back to Kent in the middle of the night.

"Do you live near here, miss?" She shook her head. She had better start talking or it might be no joke about the vagrancy. "Could I see some identification?"

She fumbled in her bag. "I'm—I'm just visiting for the weekend. I was going——" where was she going? Home, but how? "—to the bus depot."

He was wearing a uniform that identified him as city police. Not RCMP. Like Jake, she had had the naïve notion that all Canadian police were RCMP.

He studied her driver's license and her social security card, then handed them back. "You'll have a long wait for a bus this time of night."

She nodded. "I should have checked the schedule with my... my friend before I left."

"Perhaps it would be best if I drove you back to your friend's, Ms. Dalton. I think you'd have better luck with buses in the morning. You don't want to spend the night in the bus depot."

"I——" Oh, Lord! Ringing Kent's buzzer, going back. And if he thought she hadn't really meant those words spoken in the passion of making love with him, he would *know* now. Running like a crazy fool. Like Charlotte, running from Harvey, except that Harvey loved Charlotte.

"I don't want to go back. We... we had an argument." She gulped. How had she ended up in this police car, having to explain herself to this law man who sounded more concerned than officious? "If... if you could just tell me where there's a pay phone, I'll call a taxi. To go to the bus depot."

He drove her to the bus depot himself, warned her as she got out, "Next time, Ms. Dalton, don't go off in a temper in the middle of the night. You've only got to run up against the wrong man once, and your life could be ruined."

She swallowed and said sincerely, "I'm sorry—it was stupid. I—I just really wasn't thinking." She met his eyes. "I won't do it again. I'll——" she managed a smile "—I'll call a taxi before I dash out!"

He half smiled. "Or stay and make it up with your boyfriend. You'll be safe here, but why don't you phone him? He's probably tearing his hair out by now."

Phone him. There were pay telephones everywhere inside the waiting room. The place was almost empty, but there was an attendant at a ticket window and a waitress inside an empty cafeteria.

There was a clock. It was one in the morning.

She walked up to the ticket counter. She could see buses through the big double doors, but everything looked still and quiet. Didn't the buses run all through the night? Would she have to wait forever in this place? All night?

"Could you tell me when the next bus goes to...?" To where? She knew there was nothing going direct between Port Townsend and Canada. "To Seattle," she decided, knowing she could make a connection there.

"Six-fifteen."

She stared at him.

"Next one after that is eight o'clock."

Five hours. Would Kent go out looking for her when he woke and found her gone? If she had left in broad daylight, maybe not, but in the middle of the night—— Yes, probably.

Vancouver was a big enough city to get lost in, but how long would it take him to think of looking in the bus depot?

CHAPTER TEN

IT WAS three-thirty when Kent walked through the door from outside. Angela was sitting in a bolted-down seat with a plastic cup of bitter coffee in her hand. She had been studying the details of a printed leaflet that told her it would take three days to go from Vancouver to Toronto by bus. She had almost convinced herself that six-thirty would come and the bus would leave for Seattle with her on it, and Kent would not come through that door.

She jerked to look every time she heard the door. There had been an old man with a cane. Two women together. A family, the youngest child rubbing his eyes and yawning. A bus had left at two-thirty, going somewhere with about eight people on board.

More people, a scattering of yawning travelers arriving from somewhere else just after three.

Then nothing until Kent walked through the door from outside. He came two paces into the waiting room, then stopped. She watched as the door behind him slowly swung shut. He stared at her. She had thought he would be angry, but he was just cold and hard and frozen, watching her. He was not wearing the jeans and knit shirt, but his usual suit. She wondered if he would ever wear the red shirt again, and her hand went to the charm hanging from her left ear.

He jerked his head. "My car's outside. Come on."

"No. I—my bus leaves soon."

He looked around the empty waiting room. She closed her eyes, opened them again and saw the exasperation around his mouth.

"If you're so desperate to get away from me...if it can't wait until morning, I'll take you out to the airport. I don't imagine my pilot will be very happy to be dug out of bed in the middle of the night, but I'm damned if I'm leaving you here in a bloody bus depot!"

She stared at his mouth. Not the eyes, she warned herself. Keep focused on that hard mouth, and keep it together for just a few more minutes.

"I'm not coming with you. I want you to go away."

If anything, he looked more rigid, more immovable. She kept focused on that chin, hard and jutting.

"Kent, I don't want you here. I want you to go home and I'll take my bus and..." She must not cry, not until later, when she was alone, when it did not matter. "I— I don't want to see you again."

Kent and his damned sense of responsibility. She should have known. Damn it, she had known! Hadn't he always looked after Charlotte, even when she was being her most exasperating and wild? And his grandmother. Tomorrow he would be at the house she had never seen, because the woman he had called Mother all his life was upset about a neighbor painting his house blue. Even though Kent thought it was silly, he would go. Just as he had come to take charge of Charlotte's sailboat. Just as he had taken Harvey to San Francisco, because Harvey loved Charlotte and maybe it would work.

Just as he would make sure she got home safely, even though she had gone too far and blown their affair into a disaster. She saw his lips, straight and hard and turned down at the corners. She saw the muscle jump in his jaw, heard the discomfort in his voice.

"Angela, last night you said you loved me."

Something went tight and hard and painful in the pit of her stomach. He would have been smiling if she had not said those words, wanting her still. Now she was just a responsibility. She focused on his chin, but it kept going blurry. ''That was...'' She fought a spasm in her throat and somehow managed to say, ''That was just...sex.''

''It wasn't true?''

She could not manage the words. She shook her head. She felt the earrings he had given her brushing against her skin as she moved.

She held herself very still until she saw the blurry edge of the door closing behind him. Then she turned and found her way past the row of lockers, past the darkened baggage room, into the ladies' room where there was no one to see her tears.

She wouldn't have been surprised if she had turned the order of Sailing Rags from the Bellingham store into real rags, fit only for the rubbish bin. But, oddly, the pieces of canvas went together as if they knew their place without her directing them. She supposed she had her brain on autopilot, because she certainly didn't have her mind on what she was doing.

She worked from Monday until late Wednesday night, sewing alone up in the loft at the shop. Everyone left her alone. They were all unhappy with her for one reason or another. Barney was talking to her politely, as if they were strangers instead of people who had shared high school homework and Anna's apple pie. Charlotte kept talking about Kent, telling little bits and pieces of memories of the man when he was a boy, aiming the words at the middle of the room and meaning them for Angela. Harvey just looked worried, as he had back when he had been trying to trace Ben in the hope that he could put Angela's marriage back together for her, before they learned of the freeway accident.

Even Jake was sulky. Aunt Angie had forgotten to bring him even the smallest souvenir of his beloved Mounties.

She hardly noticed any of it at first, except for the flinching she felt inside whenever Charlotte said Kent's name. Her hands worked on the canvas, and her mind was stuck in some miserable mire.

Thursday morning she packed the things up and handed them over to the UPS man for delivery to Bellingham. She realized as the green truck drove away with the parcel that she had forgotten to enclose the packing slip. She sat down and wrote out the invoice and put it in an envelope, then walked out to put it in the mailbox before she forgot that too.

Sally drove up in her station wagon and rolled the window down. Wendy was beside her in a baby car seat. Jake, much to his own pleasure, was now spending his weekdays as a student at the primary school. He had told Angela the week before that he was going to be a teacher when he grew up.

Sally called, "Angie!" and Angela walked over to the car, realizing that this might be the first smile anyone had given her since last weekend.

"Hi." She had known Sally most of her life, but now she felt awkward. "Going shopping?"

"Yes—groceries. And a new dress for the dance next week. Come to dinner tomorrow?"

She nodded. Life went on. It was time she started picking up the threads. "Want a baby-sitter?" she offered.

"No, we want you. Fresh-caught salmon, done over the barbecue in our backyard. And wear something nice—I've invited our new neighbor."

She felt a sharp pain somewhere around her heart. "Sally—— "

"Angie, you've got to just grit your teeth and make yourself look for someone else. Someone who's more your own kind."

Her kind? She squeezed her eyes closed. Kent. Oh, God! Kent.

"Angie?"

She gave an odd laugh, realized that her fingers were gripping the door of Sally's station wagon. "Sally, I just can't."

Sally frowned and pushed back her soft blond hair. "You've only known him a few weeks." Sally had known Barney all her life, could not remember a time when he had been a stranger.

"Yeah." Angela stared at her fingers, gripping the window opening so hard they went white. She pulled her hands away. "It doesn't matter," she said dully. "A few weeks, or a lifetime. I've got him in my blood so bad that I seize up inside just hearing his name." The damned tears were going to come again. She blinked and said bleakly, "I'm not sure that's ever going to change. So— so don't plan any dinners with that neighbor for a while."

She walked into the shop and up the stairs and into the room where they had been leaving her alone all week. Had they talked it over, decided Sally was the envoy to come and start trying to get Angie out of herself?

They probably had a program all worked out for her. Step one was the neighbor and a neighborhood barbecue. Heaven knew what step two was. She knew they were doing it because they loved her, cared that she was hurting and did not know what to say to her.

Except Charlotte, who seemed to have worked it out that Angela was the villain. Charlotte, who always did have trouble seeing things straight.

Kent did not come for the weekend. She had known he would not, of course. Eventually he would, she supposed, to visit Charlotte, because they seemed to have formed some kind of relationship that they were both comfortable with. He did not call her Mother, but he had been talking to her and they had been laughing together.

Angela knew she would have to move. The carriage house would not be far enough. It would have to be somewhere she could not stare out and see his car in the drive. Maybe she would have to leave entirely, try to set up the Sailing Rags thing somewhere else, although there was nowhere else that was home to her.

On Monday, a letter arrived from England.

It was from her father, the words stilted and formal as they always were. The letter folded around an open airline ticket, Seattle to London, and the words, ''past time you visited us.''

How like her father to put it that way, not saying they wanted to see her. They had never been close. She had always felt that they wanted a different kind of child from the one she was. Perhaps she had never lost the resentment that had grown in that one telephone call. All those years ago. Three days after she had married Ben, standing in a telephone booth in California with Ben in the truck, impatient to be back on the road.

Her father had told her to come home at once and he would look after the divorce. The message had been plain: Ben, or her family. She had chosen her husband then, and of course her parents hadn't actually disowned her. But the feeling that they were strangers had grown, and now she stared at the letter and wondered if there was any point to using the ticket.

The ironic thing was that Kent was exactly the kind of man they would have wanted for her; yet if she did use the ticket, it would be mostly to escape Charlotte's voice saying Kent's name.

She wasn't sure what she felt about her parents. If Barney weren't so annoyed with her she would have asked his advice. She felt that there had always been strings and conditions on their love.

It took her until Wednesday to decide that she was probably going to use the ticket. It was a return ticket, and she wasn't going to stay with them more than a few days, but it would be some kind of breathing space from this place, where every time a car drove up she was tied in knots waiting for Kent to come through the door.

Her period came on Thursday, and she cried when it happened because she wanted Kent's baby growing inside her. She wished she had not gone to the doctor, had not made so sure that there would be no pregnancy. She wanted his child.

She wanted his love.

She made her announcement that night: England; her own parents; she wasn't sure how long.

Harvey said, "Angie, this is your home. You won't forget that we all love you?"

Charlotte said, "You're running away. Shouldn't you think about Kent?" Then Harvey shook his head and Charlotte said nothing more.

Angela called the travel agent and found that, while she could fly from Seattle to New York any day she wanted, she would have to wait a week for a space on the flight to London.

Barney offered to drive her into the Seatac airport for the flight and she accepted, but it took forever for the day to come. Then Barney got her there too early and they stood together in the waiting room, slightly uncomfortable with each other.

"You don't have to wait, Barney."

He shrugged, said, "I'll see you off."

"Big brother?" She managed a smile.

"Yeah. Well, you need it. The way you've been behaving lately."

"Oh," She fiddled with the tab on the zipper of her carry-on bag. "Charlotte says I'm running away."

He snorted. "Not that my scatterbrained new step-mother is in any position to criticize when it comes to running away, but that's what you're doing, isn't it?"

"I'm visiting my parents. That's not—— Oh, hell, Barney!" She closed her eyes and wailed, "I don't know what I'm doing! I forgot to wire them that I was coming."

He chewed on the inside of his cheek. "Are you sure you want to go?"

"I've got to do something, haven't I?"

He shrugged and took her arm, and at least he had stopped frowning at her. "Let's go for a coffee. And then why don't you figure out what it is that you really want? What's going to make you happy?"

She let him take her into the cafeteria. It was a Wednesday morning, and from the stream of people around them air flight was at its peak.

She drank the coffee he brought her from the counter, and decided that she was going to have to stop drinking so much coffee. The stuff was starting to taste like ashes. Everything tasted like ashes.

"Well?" asked Barney. "Have you decided?"

She shook her head and tried to smile. "Barney, being happy isn't really one of the options right now."

"Then don't you think you should think about changing your options?"

She laughed, but it didn't sound right.

He said, "Maybe Charlotte's right about more than the running."

She stared at her plastic cup and the dark liquid in it, then at Barney. Charlotte thought Kent was serious about Angela. She whispered, "You didn't think so. You told me——"

He moved impatiently. "Are you going to gamble your happiness on my being right? I hardly know the guy. You're the one who's in love with him." Barney picked up his own cup and ground out grimly, "He's not the man I would have picked for you, but you told Sally he was in your blood. Going to England isn't going to change anything if you've got it that bad."

"I know, but—I...I don't think I can face him again."

Barney laughed shortly. "Scared or miserable, take your choice."

Or scared and miserable, she thought, remembering the hard, cold line of Kent's mouth as he had stood in front of her at the bus depot.

She didn't realize that Barney had left her alone in the cafeteria until he came back. He picked up his cup without sitting down, emptied it in one long swallow of the tepid coffee.

"Your plane to New York is boarding in ten minutes."

She sighed. "I guess I'm not going." Why hadn't Kent called Charlotte? Charlotte had expected him to call, and he had no reason not to. Unless...

That harsh, freezing look from the bus depot. The same message that had been in his eyes back on the sea wall when he'd told her he had no practice with relationships. She had thought he was saying that he did not want a relationship with her. All that weekend, she had been so afraid he would tell her she had no real place in his life.

What if that was wrong? What if she had gone to him, touched his chest and looked into his eyes, looked for something behind the ice in his eyes? Was it possible that he was frightened too? That he...loved her?

"There's a flight to Vancouver leaving in twenty minutes." Barney frowned and said, "Or do you want me to drive you up there?"

"No." She bit her lip. "It's going to be bad enough without witnesses."

"I'll track down your luggage for you," he offered.

"What?"

"Your suitcase. It's checked through to London. Don't worry about it, I'll look after it."

Her luggage was the last thing she was worried about. She had never been quite so frightened in all her life. Kent might not let her in. Even if he did, he would quite likely not want to hear what she had to say. She would have to speak her piece in cold blood . . . watch his eyes. She would know if she watched his eyes.

The plane. She got on, then somehow missed the part where it took off. Suddenly the flight attendant was hovering over her, asking quietly, "Are you nervous? It's going to be a quiet flight."

Angela shook her head. "Thanks, I'm fine."

In Vancouver, the Canadian Customs officer took her birth certificate and asked if she was visiting for business or pleasure. She said pleasure, and he looked at her oddly. She wondered if she looked as frightened as she felt.

She went to the currency exchange window and changed a hundred dollars into Canadian. Then she went to a telephone booth, found a listing for Ferguson Holdings in a telephone book and walked outside to the row of waiting taxis.

CHAPTER ELEVEN

KENT'S office suite was what Angela would have expected—quiet, elegant, expensive. Eleven floors higher than the rest of the world. The receptionist matched the décor, dark-haired, immaculate and expensive. Angela walked up to the desk and tried to look as if she belonged.

"I'd like to see Mr. Ferguson, please."

The brunette smiled with professional regret. "Mr. Ferguson is completely booked. Perhaps I could help you?"

A door burst open behind her and a slight, worried man rushed out, closed the door quietly, then dropped a small pile of papers on the receptionist's desk with quiet violence.

He spoke to the receptionist in a low-voiced tirade, his voice trembling with anger. "Patricia, the man's impossible! What's got into him lately? Look what he's asking for! I tell you, those elevations are all wrong!"

The brunette turned away from Angela and spoke soothingly, her voice so low that Angela could barely hear. "David, do what you can. He's not in a very good mood today, but I'm sure——"

The thin man muttered, "If Kent pulls one more of these tantrums on me he can find himself another architect!"

Kent throwing tantrums? Kent? Angela's hand moved absently to touch one of the earrings she had been wearing ever since Kent had put them in her ears. Her fingers toyed with the little golden bird.

The receptionist and the architect were talking together in low, intense voices. Angela took a deep breath, then stole quietly past them. She reached for the knob to the closed door and opened it, slipping inside.

Kent was standing at a window overlooking the ocean. She shut the door and leaned against it, her hands flat against the door behind her back. He swung around and she felt her fingers go into tight fists, nails digging into her palms.

"Patricia, tell that——"

His voice stopped abruptly. The light from the window turned him into nothing more than a silhouette. He was staring at her, she could tell that much, and that there was a big desk between them. She moved forward— one step, then another. Something on his desk buzzed and he moved, leaned over and pushed the intercom.

"Yes, Patricia?"

"Mr. Harmon on line one, returning your call."

He snapped, "No calls."

The intercom said, "What about your luncheon appointment with the Tredway consortium?"

"Cancel it."

He had not said a word to Angela, but he had not taken his eyes off her either. He came around his desk, walking slowly and deliberately. He was halfway across the carpet before she managed to find her voice.

"Don't! Kent..."

He stopped abruptly. She was not sure what it was in his eyes, but it was *something*.

She gulped. "I—I came to... to say something." She licked her lips and wondered where all the words were that she had practiced on the jet. His tie was askew. She had never seen him looking so messy before. She swallowed and blurted, "My parents want me to come to England."

He rammed his hands into his pockets. "Is that what you came to tell me? You're going away?"

She shook her head dumbly.

A muscle jumped along the side of his jaw and the colour abruptly left his face. "Are you pregnant?"

She shook her head. It was a good thing she wasn't. He looked sick at the thought. What was she doing here? She closed her eyes and even then she could see him standing, waiting. She whispered, "Just now, why did you cancel your lunch?"

"Angela! Say it, whatever it is, or God help me I'll shake it out of you!"

Her eyes flew open and he was glaring at her angrily. He made an angry sound and she met his eyes. Say it. She wasn't sure if she could. She gulped and whispered, "I—I came because I . . . because I love you."

Everything went still—his body, his face, his eyes, blue gone to black. "What did you just say?"

She closed her eyes. She had thought she would know from his eyes. "I—I lied when I said I . . . when I said I didn't mean it."

His mouth opened, but no sound came. He shook his head. "I—— Damn it, Angela! If——" He swung away from her, prowled to the window, then spun back to demand, "Why did you run away? Why?"

She licked her lips and his eyes flashed. Her heart started beating again. "Because—because I love you . . . and I wasn't supposed to say it. It was supposed to be . . . and you didn't, and I——"

"Angela!" She jerked at his shout and his voice dropped abruptly to a whisper. "I didn't what?"

"Love me." She studied his chin, then made herself meet his eyes because, if this was it, she didn't want any doubts left to torment herself with.

"You——" His voice broke. "Oh, you idiot! Come here."

He didn't wait for her to come, but crossed the few feet between them and pulled her into his arms. She felt the shudder go through his body as he held her close. She pushed her hands against his chest so that she could see his face clearly, his eyes.

His eyes blazed hot and blue and he ground out, "You crazy fool! How the hell could you not know? It must have been obvious to everyone from here to Port Townsend that I—I'm nuts about you!"

He loved her. Of course he loved her. It was in his eyes, had been in his eyes always. She stretched up on her toes and touched his lips with hers. The harshness left his lips and he took her mouth with a deep invasion that left her clinging.

When he lifted his head she realized that the ringing in her ears came from somewhere behind him. The intercom. He ignored it, kissed her again, softer, teasing, then possessing.

When he finally let her lips go, he said harshly, "I've been going insane. Over two weeks, and I've spent most of that time thinking about calling you, going to you. I thought——" He held her close, hard, and said bleakly, "I thought if I could see you, I could make you change your mind. After all, I've done it before."

"Yes." She turned her face into his shoulder, felt the hard thud of his heart. "Why didn't you?"

He threaded his hands up through her hair, drew her head back so that he could look into her eyes. "Because if you really didn't want to be with me, if I seduced you into it against your will...it wouldn't be any good, darling. I couldn't face a life of wondering if you were leaving me every time you were out of my sight."

Her heart stopped. "A life?"

She threaded her fingers through his hair and managed to make it even more of a mess than he had earlier. He closed his eyes and she saw his face go bleak and empty.

"The night you ran away," he said in a low, ragged voice. "After we made love, I went to sleep with you in my arms, thinking you were mine forever... and I woke up alone. God, Angela, I went insane worrying, looking for you, thinking of the things that could have happened to you! Alone in a strange city! And Saturday night, all the crazies out drinking! You——"

"I'm sorry," she said softly. "I was afraid. I—I'd just realized how much I loved you, and—and after—I was afraid you'd wake up and—I thought—I—you wouldn't want it."

He took her face with his hands, whispered, "When I look at you, when I touch you, it's the only thing in my mind. I wanted to tell you, but somehow... I don't know why it was so hard. I love you. I've never said those words to another woman. You're the only woman I've ever loved." His voice went hoarse and he said, "Don't ever forget that, because without you the rest of my life is nothing more than a wasteland."

She turned her face to kiss his hand and she felt him tremble, then his arms dropped away from her, leaving her standing alone.

"Will you stay, Angela? Will you stay with me?"

She met his eyes and promised, "As long as you want me."

"Be sure, Angela."

"I'm sure."

He stood silently, studying her eyes, reading what was in her heart, not hiding any of his deep love for this woman who had changed his life from emptiness into loving.

He lifted her hands up to his lips. "Ever since I left you in that bus depot, I've been haunted by the things I'd wanted to share with you. I wanted everything—to be able to come to you, wherever you are, and know you would look up and smile when you saw me. To wake with you in my arms, every day. You're the only woman I've ever wanted to find in my arms when I wake up. I—will you have my children?"

"Yes," she whispered. "Please. Our children."

"Oh, yes, darling... ours." He breathed in the warm scent of her. "You'd have to marry me."

"Mmm." She shivered and smiled. "Soon, I hope?"

He laughed. She loved the sound of his laughter. "Very soon. We'll have to find a house for the children—something out of the city. Port Townsend, if you'd like."

"I——" She closed her eyes and felt the tears welling up. "I thought—— Don't you need to live in the city? Your work?"

"The only thing I need is you." He moved his lips to kiss away the moisture at her eyes. "With telephones and computers and the Lear, I can easily look after everything from Port Townsend." He grinned and offered, "Or Alaska, for that matter."

"No, Port Townsend will do fine. I——" She would have gone anywhere with him if he had asked.

She reached up to kiss him, but he stopped her, covering her lips with his fingers. "That's dangerous, you know. I keep telling myself I should have some self-control, but every time I kiss you——"

"I know," she whispered, moving closer into his arms. "I'm counting on that... Kiss me, my love."

On the desk, the intercom buzzed.

He took her into his arms, his lips telling her of his love with shattering persuasion.

The office door opened with a quiet whoosh on the carpet.

"Excuse me, Kent, but—oh! I——"

He lifted his head, holding Angela tightly in his arms. "Patricia, get out, and lock the door behind you."

Angela heard a choked sound, then, "But what about—shall I cancel the——?"

"Do what you like, just get out." Kent dropped his eyes to Angela's and added, "Cancel whatever needs canceling, just leave me alone with the woman I'm going to marry. And——"

"I know. Lock the door." A click, then the door closing, locked.

Kent stared down at the woman he loved, his hands moving on her back, caressing, lips against her mouth, confessing, "No one's ever done what you do to me. I warned you what would happen if I kissed you."

Her heart was singing. She smiled and pulled him closer, whispering, "Kiss me again . . . don't ever stop."

HARLEQUIN ROMANCE®

**Harlequin Romance
knows love can be dangerous!**

Don't miss
TO LOVE AND PROTECT (#3223)
by Kate Denton,
the October title in

THE BRIDAL COLLECTION

THE GROOM'S life was in peril.
THE BRIDE was hired to help him.
BUT THEIR WEDDING was *more* than
a business arrangement!

Available this month in
The Bridal Collection
JACK OF HEARTS (#3218)
by Heather Allison
Wherever Harlequin books are sold.

WED-6

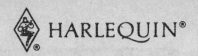

JAYNE ANN KRENTZ

Dreams
Parts One & Two

The warrior died at her feet, his blood running out of the cave entrance and mingling with the waterfall. With his last breath he cursed the woman— told her that her spirit would remain chained in the cave forever until a child was created and born there....

So goes the ancient legend of the Chained Lady and the curse that bound her throughout the ages—until destiny brought Diana Prentice and Colby Savager together under the influence of forces beyond their understanding. Suddenly they were both haunted by dreams that linked past and present, while their waking hours were filled with danger. Only when Colby, Diana's modern-day warrior, learned to love, could those dark forces be vanquished. Only then could Diana set the Chained Lady free....

WELCOME TO

The quintessential small town, where everyone
knows everybody else!

Finally, books that capture the pleasure
of tuning in to your favorite TV show!

Join your friends at Tyler in the eighth book, BACHELOR'S PUZZLE by Ginger
Chambers, available in October.

*What do Tyler's librarian and a cosmopolitan architect have in common? What
does the coroner's office have to reveal?*

GREAT READING...GREAT SAVINGS...
AND A FABULOUS FREE GIFT!

Each book set in Tyler is a self-contained love story; together, the twelve novels
stitch the fabric of the community. You can't miss the Tyler books on the shelves
because the covers honor the old American tradition of quilting; each cover
depicts a patch of the large Tyler quilt!

And you can receive a FABULOUS GIFT, ABSOLUTELY FREE, by collecting
proofs-of-purchase found in each Tyler book, *and* use our Tyler coupons to save
on your next TYLER book purchase.

If you missed *Whirlwind* (March), *Bright Hopes* (April), *Wisconsin Wedding* (May), *Monkey
Wrench* (June), *Blazing Star* (July), *Sunshine* (August) or *Arrowpoint* (September) and would
like to order them, send your name, address, zip or postal code, along with a check or money
order for $3.99 (please do not send cash), plus 75¢ postage and handling ($1.00 in Canada)
for each book ordered, payable to Harlequin Reader Service, to:

In the U.S.	In Canada
3010 Walden Avenue	P.O. Box 609
P.O. Box 1325	Fort Erie, Ontario
Buffalo, NY 14269-1325	L2A 5X3

Please specify book title(s) with your order.
Canadian residents add applicable federal and provincial taxes.   TYLER-8